Dragon Train
Book I

RJ the Story Guy

High Desert Libris

Albuquerque

Copyright © 2020 by **RJ the Story Guy**

All rights reserved. No part of this publication may be reproduced, distributed or transmitted in any form or by any means, without prior written permission.

High Desert Libris
Albuquerque, NM

Publisher's Note: This is a work of fiction. Names, characters, places, and incidents are a product of the author's imagination. Locales and public names are sometimes used for atmospheric purposes. Any resemblance to actual people, living or dead, or to businesses, companies, events, institutions, or locales is completely coincidental.

Book Layout © 2017 BookDesignTemplates.com
Cover Art by Celebril, found at https://celebrilart.com/
Book Design by Paul Murray, found at http://gpmurray.com

Dragon Train/RJ the Story Guy. -- 1st ed.
ISBN 978-1-7334361-2-0

This is for the Young in Spirit
whose Dragon Hearts beat strong

Special Thanks to:
Kathy Waggoner
Joyce Hertzoff
For their intelligent and insightful
Editing and suggestions
That turned a fair manuscript into
One I proudly share with readers.
Thanks to:
Celebril and
Paul Murray for their artistic vision.

Thanks to my wife whose support and love makes it all possible.

CONTENTS

Face to Face 1
Still Alive 12
A Walk in the Forest 22
Hang On! 31
The Cave of the Dragon 35
Dark Cloud's Tale 41
A Little Dragon Chemistry 46
Dark Cloud's Family on the Farm 51
Sadness in the Cave 66
Stuck in the Center of the Earth 75
The End of Dark Cloud's Story 84
The Problem with Hawks 93
Birds and Dragons of a Feather 101
Skye and Caerulus 109
Bait and Switch 122
Unscheduled Stopover 131
Tricky Footing 139
Free at Last! 149
Country Boy in the Big City 158
Best Laid Plans of Dragons and Men 171
The Circle Shall be Unbroken 187
Well-Placed Rocks 195
Homecoming 204

ONE

Face to Face

I don't remember the Eastbound Dragon Train ever stopping in Hilltop. Grownups around here say it never happened in their lifetimes. Maybe Grandma Kesterson might have seen it but she was nearly a hundred years old and could barely recall what she did five minutes ago.

But that didn't matter when I walked out of the barn. I had just finished milking all but the last two cows in our herd like a thousand times before. I carried a bucket of warm milk steaming in the cold morning air.

That's when the sound of the dragon's deep breathing reached my ears. I looked across the long stretch from our farm on the ridge toward Hilltop. The Dragon Train was climbing to the top of Long Hill just before passing through town. Nothing new about that.

But this morning those dragon puffs were loud, sounding like Grandma hacking and coughing while she smoked a hand-rolled cigarette. That got my attention. I watched as the train appeared outside of town.

The train was barely moving. The dragon dipped low plowing dirt and gravel as it strained to flap its big wings.

Usually the train picked up speed when the dragon screeched as if relieved the hard work was done. Heading on down from dinky Hilltop to the big city of Portville, it was an easy coast from the hills. But this faded old blue dragon could hardly manage a wheezy cough as the train lost speed.

When I saw the Dragon Train slowing, I completely forgot what I was doing and dashed for the train station in the center of Hilltop. I ran across our yard, passed our little wooden house and towards the stone fence that marked the border between us and our neighbors.

Wait a minute! As I climbed over the fence, something occurred to me. I looked back at the barn door. The milk bucket that I just had in my hand was now turned over on the ground.

Dad'll give me what-for when he finds a big puddle of fresh milk on the cold ground between the barn and our shack.

No time for that! As I turned to head down the hill, I instinctively slapped my left hip checking to make sure I had my leather pouch with a skinning knife, an ancient leather cord slingshot, and smooth river rocks. None!

I turned back to the barn. I had to make time to get the pouch because I might have to sling a rock between the dragon's eyes if he got out of line. Yeah, right, whatever. Still, I felt better prepared with my farmer boy weapons.

I tore along the hill's narrow pathways and cut through barren gardens, pretty sure our neighbors wouldn't mind since it was time for spring planting. And if they did mind, oh well.

A Dragon Train stopping! Here! My only chance to see a real dragon up close. Not from *way* up on the valley's ridge when they flash by in a few moments looking more like a flying squirrel pulling a train of wooden toy cars.

Reaching the creek, I let gravity speed my flying feet as I leaped across the water and landed a foot short of the opposite bank. Oh, man, the cold water went right through my worn-out boots. The icy bite hurt, but I didn't care.

At the bottom of the hill, I ran across the village square, around the broken-down train station and bounded up the creaking steps. I looked up the tracks.

Sure enough, the Dragon Train limped along. The large blue beast flew a few feet above the tracks as it weaved back and forth straining to pull the train another hundred yards to the loading platform.

I knew it! The train was going to stop in Hilltop.

If it didn't stop, the great beast would die before reaching our poor train station. Delivering mail was the only thing our station was good for long before I was born.

The beat-up leather mailbags were left off and picked up from giant hooks that stood by the station. The trains barely slowed as one bag from the train caught on the incoming hook and, on the other side of the train car, the outgoing bag was unhooked and carried off as the train sped for Portville.

Just as the blue beast's ribs heaved to draw in fresh cold air, the dragon collapsed on the tracks. Its wings spanning wider than the size of any home in Hilltop, settled down like old quilts tossed on a bed.

By the size of him, my little river rocks wouldn't do. I needed a rock the size of our old bull's head to bring this beast down. Oh, well.

"Is he dead?" I asked the postman who watched this drama from the edge of the loading platform.

"Naw, Jaiden, not yet. Lookit its nostrils. Still openin' and closin' trying to draw breath, though I don't think it'll be long for this world..."

I watched the dragon not more than five feet away. The ragged edges of its nostrils came together as the monster sucked in barrels of air and then blew out a stench smelling like rotten eggs.

"Phew! That's gross!" I said. "Smells worse than a struck match or my old dog's farts."

"That's the sulfur in their blood system that used to allow them to spew fire, though this beast couldn't light a hanky with what little air it has left." The old postman shook his head. "A waste of a perfectly good dragon!" he said and turned to go back into the station.

With the large wooden train cars drawn to a halt behind the fallen beast, a conductor in a wrinkled red coat, black cap and pants jumped to the ground out of the lead car and ran to the postman.

"You have to send an emergency message—"

"What'ya think I'm doing right now?" the postman said. "Going to mend my socks? Of course, I'm fixin' to scratch a message and send my old pigeon hen to Portville right now. Last time I sent a message was a year ago when the Eastbound flew past here with a wheel 'bout ready to fall off the caboose's axles!"

"Oh," the conductor said, a bit flustered. "That's fine. Uh, thank you."

The postman grumbled and disappeared into the station house.

The conductor walked over to the suffering dragon and kicked it in the ribs. "You dad-blamed old fool cow! Couldn't even pull us down the hills to the city. Now we'll have to cut you loose and let you rot right here in the middle of Hilltop." He groaned and shrugged his shoulders.

Turning to the gathering crowd, he announced, "When we saw this blamed dragon struggling, I knew we should've thrown it off the cliff back a ways and let her carcass feed the wild animals of the forest! 'Course we wouldn't have even made it this far without a dragon to pull the train. Sorry stinkin' beast!"

He unbuckled the harness that attached the dragon to the shafts connected to the lead car. I caught sight of the train pilot pacing back and forth in his tiny cab. He flung his dragon whip back and forth like he was killing a snake. Maybe he was aggravated he couldn't flog the blue giant to pull the train just far enough to coast to Portville, fifty long miles away.

I couldn't imagine fifty miles when the farthest I ever been was seven miles away from town during hunting season.

This is the only time I ever got this near to a train-towing dragon, and now all I get is watching this poor old wreck breathe its last. Somehow, it didn't seem right.

I jumped off the platform and circled the great beast's head which was about the size of the kitchen in our house. The dragon's breath smelled even worse and burned my throat.

Massive eyes, as big as a ten-gallon bucket, opened slightly and looked in my direction, though it seemed like it didn't really see me. After a few moments, the eyes widened and a liveliness sparkled as the dragon must have realized a human was looking into its depths.

The dragon sucked in more air than I thought possible for an animal so near death. Then I heard something I never expected.

Are you the dragonherder come to lead me to my rest in the Caverns of Heaven? Or do I deserve no more than the Firepits of Hell?

Was that the dragon's wheezing voice? Dragons don't talk! But if this one did, it wouldn't sound like a woman. Would it?

Will I join my father and the mother who tended my egg along with those of my brothers and sisters? What about my siblings who may be dead? And my darling babies who have never flown? Will I at last curl around my loved ones and rest eternally?

"Uh…" was all I could mumble. What was I supposed to say? A talking dragon? And what in the world was it talking about? Like it was some kind of human facing death and longing for rest in Heaven, as if it had a soul?

Grownups in the crowd, started talking all at once.

"What was that? Did you hear something?"

"No… well, I heard wheezing and a whispering like someone talking—a woman, I think."

"What did the voice say and where did it come from?"

"Is it a ghost?" Someone asked. And so, the questions flew around the crowd.

I looked at the dragon and wondered what a dragon would say if it could talk. And if it could, would it talk about Heaven of all places? How could a dumb beast, only fit for towing trains across the mountains and prairies of Nulland, expect to rest in some kind of dragon heaven—or any kind of heaven for that matter?

More craziness.

But the creature couldn't have spoken.

Dragons don't talk!

The crowd murmured in a way that was more threatening than the stories about a weyr of Dragons back in the old days. Back then, my father told me, dragons had not been broken of their wild ways. Now, they were used for transportation and war machines.

"Somebody's messing around with us like we're dumb country bumpkins," a voice spat.

Old Joal, one of farmers who lived just a hill away from us took a long hard look at the dragon. "Maybe that dragon is possessed or something," he said.

"Yeah," said his wife beside him. "Joal, you could be right. The least that beast has done is scare a lot of us folks making them weird noises."

"Who cares if it is dying," the village baker said. "We need to finish it off and—"

I could tell by the way the conductor peered into the crowd's faces, that he feared violence from the crowd. He turned to face the postman. "It's bad enough we have a broken-down dead dragon on our hands and now we've got a riot brewing?" he muttered, as if expecting the postman, to control the crowd.

"Don't go lookin' at me to solve your problems. All your bunch does is whip through our little village, grab our mail and leave off a few goods we can't find in our sad excuse for a store. As it is, the store owner has to ride a wagon for five hard days on rocky roads to get to Portville for essentials twice a year."

"Aw, quit your complaining. It's not our fault your village is so little it's not even worth a stop once a month—"

"This problem is your'uns, not mine or any of these forsaken souls here. Clean up your own dead dragon mess." The postman glared at the fidgeting conductor, spit on the ground near the trainman's black polished shoes, and headed through the crowd to his cramped post office.

Over his shoulder, the postman snarled, "I'll go send your gall-darned message while you cool your heels back in your comfy office on the train."

"It's about time," the conductor said. "Tell 'em that blamed Number 4 has given up the ghost and they need to send a crew to collect the body." He turned on his heel and began a fast walk back to the train.

I got a little scared as the crowd shifted on their feet. Would they jump the conductor before he made his way to the lead train car? His eyes still looked fearful though he put on a tough face as he grimaced and snarled at me as if all this was my fault. The conductor ignored the restless townspeople and rushed toward the train to wait for the rescue operation from Portville.

Yeah, pick on the young guy in the crowd with your dirty looks, I thought. When he reached the lead car, he quickly closed the door and I heard the lock clank.

Hilltop was small and I often heard people complain about being stuck here for the rest of their lives. There was no one else who had a higher position in the town than the postman. In a way, he was sticking up for us against the stuffed shirt conductor in his red coat and the whole Dragon Train business.

He trotted back to his dusty little post office and didn't quite close the door all the way. The people milled around for a few minutes, grumbling among themselves and spitting until they slowly began leaving the station to return to their boring chores.

I'm sure, like me, they came to the station, fascinated and curious. But now I could tell by people's expressions that the dying dragon and the grouchy conductor squeezed the excitement from the hearts of all who came.

As some of the village people were departing, my father tramped down the hill. I scooted around behind the crowd, staying out of his line of sight. Chatting with Old Joal, he got the gist of what had happened. Within a couple of minutes, there I was, exposed, no crowd to hide behind.

I froze as he walked toward me. I could feel his anger like a hot stove in a cold room.

"What are you doing, Jaiden? There's two more cows to be milked and goats to feed before you can even think about supper. Get on home!"

I almost talked back to him, but stopped myself just short of outright disobedience. "Oh, okay, but can't I stay just a little longer? This poor dragon still breathes."

My father gave the blue monster a hard look, its breathing now much slower and weaker. "What's the point? You want to adopt it and have it eat us out of house and home so you can have an oversized *pet?* For someone fifteen years old you can be so stupid! Let it die. It's the railroad's problem, not ours."

"But, Dad..."

"Don't 'But Dad' me," he roared. "I've spoken, now you get up the hill and finish your work."

I knew better than to say anymore or even give him my "you-can't-make-me" look. With a quick glance back at the dragon—it's eyes now shut and breathing much slower—I followed my father back to the ridge to our small grazing fields and broken-down barn.

I picked up the overturned bucket, wiped the cold mud off, and headed for the trough to wash it before milking the two remaining cows of our tiny herd. I couldn't help but look back down to the center of town.

In the aging night, the black form of the dying dragon was hardly visible on the tracks. Soon there would be only darkness in the heart of Hilltop and silence as the great lungs of the beast breathed their last.

TWO

Still Alive

Morning came, not with light and the warm rays of the sun but with deep blackness and the hard bite of frost. I wanted to cry and drop back into a deep sleep but I pulled out of bed as if my Dad had come in and dragged me into the cold night to feed the animals and turn the hay in their stalls.

Outside, a billion stars winked at me and the lonely town below. I stopped just outside the barn and listened. A few animals inside snorted and rustled about ready for my entrance which meant food and fresh water.

From my place high above the valley I listened like a guard dog focusing his attention, on the alert for invaders. There was nothing—

No, wait. There was something. A slow but regular sigh. Not weak, but sure and alive. The dragon? Could it be? After all that had happened late yesterday, was it still alive? But how could I hear it from this far away?

My father stuck his head out the tiny kitchen window. "What the blue blazes are you waiting for? Feed the animals and take care of them like you're supposed to or I'll move your bed into the barn so you don't have to go so far to do your duties."

Slam him! I wanted to run down the hill, but I knew not even the tiniest bit of forgiveness lurked in my father's heart, so I rushed into the barn before he came out with a leather strap in his hand.

Most of the time, he never went through with threats of a whipping, but when he did… And now with this dragon business the day before, he was not in the most forgiving mood.

Later, after a hot bowl of sticky oatmeal and stale coffee, I would milk the cows as fast as I could, release them to the pasture and run back to the station.

Surely, I was dreaming and the dragon was long dead, but what if it wasn't? Finding the beast still alive would be worth even a blistered hind end when Dad found out…

I flew like the wind through morning chores, left two brimming buckets of milk just outside the barn door, and stole away hiding among the cows until I reached the low end of the pasture. The faster I ran, the better chance I had of reaching the train station unseen by Dad.

I stopped on the station platform. It just occurred to me that I still should have my slingshot. Slapped my left hip. Yep, still there.

Afraid that beyond the railroad tracks was a frozen dragon body, I avoided looking until I crawled along the ground and crossed the tracks.

I finally raised my eyes, heart pounding so hard against my ribs I thought it would jump out of my chest.

But before my eyes focused on the giant carcass in the dim light of dawn, I heard a sound like the huge bellows of our town's blacksmith.

The dragon was breathing strong and deep.

Suddenly unafraid, I ran to the big head. Those eyes, like glass globes, opened and looked at me without surprise or anger.

"You're still alive," I said, immediately realizing how stupid that sounded.

Of course, the dragon wasn't going to answer because dragons don't speak, but the massive head seemed to nod slightly. For the first time, I noticed the color of the dragon's eyes, golden with brown flecks like old copper floating around the black slit of its pupils.

Not wanting to stare into those eyes, I ran around the beast's prone body looking for wounds and broken limbs. Finding none, I came back to the head and, like an idiot, spoke again.

"I don't see anything wrong with you. But you must still be very tired. What can a punk like me do to help you?"

Again, not anxious to look into those eyes, I glanced around, desperate to see something, *anything* that might help get the dragon on its feet and then...

Then what? Cow manure! What do I do with a sick dragon? In the middle of Hilltop? All too soon, people from the railroad company would be here to check on the dragon. Did that mean they would nurse it back to health, or put it down because they didn't want the trouble of dealing with a sick beast?

I had a hunch they wanted to save themselves any trouble. But if it was still alive and—maybe—could get better... My dad always scolded me when I wanted to save one of our animals when all he wanted was to get on with running the farm.

I had many nightmares seeing the pleading, suffering eyes of some cow or goat or my last dog a few minutes before Dad had decided to do the "humane thing" as he called it. It wasn't very humane for me. He called me a cry-baby more than once. "You're just like your sob-sister mother. Grow up!" he would say.

Maybe I was a cry-baby. I was only two when Mom died. I have no memory of her except in my imagination and the two faded drawings Dad kept on his nightstand. He never talked about her so I wondered if he loved her or if his constant bad mood was because she left him to raise me alone.

Still, she must of have been more than a sob-sister to him if he kept her pictures where she was the last thing he saw at night and the first thing in the morning.

Whatever. I had a problem to solve.

I looked to the east to gauge how much longer before daybreak. Not long. Less than a half hour. Then some of the townspeople would start to stir and go outdoors if only to make a trip to their outhouses.

How could I hide a dragon?

That was my silent thought, but a woman's hoarse voice answered. *Take me into the forest beyond those trees.* The dragon lifted its tail. Was it pointing?

Feeling stupid, I followed the motion of the tail and looked at a clump of trees a couple of hundred yards to the south of the tracks. Beyond lay the thick Emerald Forest where it would be hard to find a dragon, that is if one could squeeze such a large beast between the trees.

My mind blank and heart pounding, I finally looked back at the dragon. I watched its face as I asked, "Did you just say that and then point to the Emerald Forest?"

Who else is here? The lips didn't move, but I heard the voice both in my head and, sort of, from her mouth. That can't be right!

"Dragons can't talk!" I shouted.

Shush! Only you and I now know that's not true. So, keep quiet if you want to help me.

Okay, so what else am I supposed to think? I gave it up for now as my mind moved to the next thing that popped up.

"Excuse me, uh, dragon, but your voice sounds a little higher pitched than I would expect. That is, if a dragon could, or uh, for a dragon that *seems* to speak—"

No time for that. Please help me up.

"What? Really? How can I lift a great big dragon?"

I'll get myself up, but you can help me keep from falling. Grab hold of my wing right there by your feet and pull me towards you so I can keep my balance. I still feel woozy.

"Woozy? What are you, a clown dragon? Making jokes—"

Pardon me, but be quiet and do as I ask if you wish to help.

I couldn't stop myself from mumbling much like I did when my father made some ridiculous request and my arguing was pointless.

I grabbed the wing by its leading edge and marveled at the thin, soft skin stretched over graceful arching bones. I looked back at the dragon. "Ready?"

Ready, young man. Pull!

I pulled and the dragon rocked itself towards me curling its muscular legs under itself. Now the beast was on its stomach.

Once again, the now gentler voice of the dragon said.

I gave a mighty—at least for me-—pull as the dragon swung upright so swiftly it almost continued over on top of me!

There. Good. You can let go of my wing. I don't feel like flying, but I want to fold my wings on my back. Makes walking easier.

I let go. I couldn't believe it as the wings rose like the sails of a great sailing ship and folded delicately on the dragon's back.

Now release me from the straps, the beast said.

I followed the straps of the harness around its neck and shoulders past a small saddle bag, then along the heavy wooden shaft connected with chains to more straps wound around the dragon. The chain links were thicker than my arms. Now how was I going to cut or loosen anything? *Don't worry about how hard this is going to be,* the dragon said. *Just look where straps lead up to the pilot's box on the lead car.*

I did and saw how inside the pilot's box, block and tackle pulleys were threaded with ropes to give the pilot more power as he guided the dragon. The rings at the dragon's end of the ropes were merely looped through rings on the straps that connected to the harness and bridle on the dragon. At the other end, straps from the pulleys were held by the pilot as he guided the dragon.

I was impressed with how clever that was. Dad and I would use pulleys to lift heavy bales of hay to store on the top levels of our barn and to lift the wagon when he had to take off the wheels to grease the hubs.

Anyhow, these connections of straps, harnesses and ropes were impossible for a dragon to release without having hands but not hard at all for a guy like myself. Especially since I was used to working with all kinds of hooks, straps, bolts, and rope around the farm.

"OK," I said as I released the straps and took a deep breath. "If you want me to get this harness off, that's going to take longer."

Never mind about the harness, the dragon said.

"Well, come on, follow me."

What a pair we made strolling on a worn path and soon disappearing into the bushes! Crazy. So far no one had caught the unbelievable sight until—

"What the—?" an old man's voice shouted immediately to our left.

Both of us turned to see old Henry standing outside his shack in the half-light holding a bedside pail.

I thought fast. "Oh. Good morning, Mr. Henry. Fine morning isn't it? I just finished milking our cows and my Dad sent me down with the horse," I motioned toward the dragon as if it *were* my horse, "to get a bag of oats for the animals. I had forgotten yesterday with all the excitement about the dead dragon."

The old man looked carefully at me then shifted his gaze upward at the dragon who seemed to take on the facial expression of a sleepy-head old horse. Of course, it was a little too tall for any kind of horse. Mr. Henry shook his head hard and rubbed his eyes.

I motioned to the dragon to hurry towards the clump of trees ahead. I looked back and saw the old man quit rubbing his eyes and look at me with an expression of astonishment.

"Your horse? Jaiden, where'd your horse go?"

"Oh, you know these farm animals. All they want to do is get back to their stall to sleep and eat unless we put a harness on them and put them to work." I tried to smile though I didn't feel very amused.

The man formed his lips as if to say, "oh," but merely nodded and slowly turned toward his outhouse to dump the evening's contents from his bedside pail.

As I followed along behind the dragon, I heard Mr. Henry mumble, "I'll be hog-tied and horse-whipped. That dad-blamed beast dying by the tracks has my mind in an uproar. Best to go about my business and let my brain clear itself of such foolishness!" He chuckled.

Boy, was I relieved.

Meanwhile the dragon and I reached the safety of the Emerald Forest without any more problems.

I looked down the path villagers had worn over the centuries as they sought game for hunting and fresh water from the river. The path was surrounded by trees crowded in too close for a dragon to make its way through.

"What do we do now?" I asked and looked square into the dragon's eyes as it dipped its big head by me. Those golden eyes with the coppery flecks froze me in place. The dragon's intense look bore right through me like I was made of butter.

Though I am quite large, I am as flexible as any other reptile. Though, I do think I'm a lot smarter. Lead the way, I'll follow—

"Are you sure about this? Do I look that stupid?" I said to the dragon which still seemed to not move its lips while a strangely high-pitched voice resounded in my head.

No, of course not. You are a clever farmer boy who wants a little more from life than tending cows and cutting weeds in the garden. But right now, there is no time for argument. Go. I'll follow.

So, I went. After a few steps I turned and was startled to find the beast right behind me, its breath blowing in my face. I leaned right and then left looking past the huge head and saw that the dragon had sucked in those mighty ribs and wasn't much wider than I was.

The big head rose up, I followed that motion until my head tilted all the way back.

"You're so much taller than me and yet you can suck in your ribs that much?"

As I said, reptiles are flexible.

"A couple of other things, since we're discussing you. Do you have a name? And what are you—a boy or a girl?"

Neither. I am an adult, many years—actually decades—older than you. I have children of my own. I'm probably older than your father since we dragons live at least two centuries.

"Boy or girl?" I insisted.

I am a female—not girl—dragon. My name is Skye and I have given birth to dozens of hatchlings, but... The big voice in my head seemed to choke up. *All my babies lived or died in chains, like the chains that bound me to the train. I have three hatchlings left. I am so tired. I want to fly free.*

I couldn't think of a thing to say and my voice was throttled in my throat like I had swallowed a big apple.

What's your name? she asked.

"Jaiden."

Good name, but I may not have long, I'm afraid, she said. *I felt like I was dying pulling the train uphill to your village. I am grateful you cut me loose. But I'm not ready to die just yet. I need more time...*

I still couldn't speak, so I turned and continued on the path. The dragon's heavy footsteps followed behind me as we passed deeper into the forest. The dark silence ruled all, even my mind.

THREE

A Walk in the Forest

Past mid-morning, I heard dogs baying in the distance. Did I just imagine it?

No, you didn't, Jaiden, she said. I was a little startled she knew what I thought.

The railroad people are here. I guess I'm not the first dragon to attempt an escape after collapsing. They must have sent hounds along with their people. I can fool them, but I need your help.

"What can I do?" She was clearly desperate but I didn't know how to hide an animal as big as Skye, much less myself.

Take us to the nearest meadow or even a clearing a few feet wide will do.

"I haven't spent much time in this place. We're all a little afraid of the forest because there's stories with all sorts of weird animals living in here."

No excuses! Certainly, you know it a little better than I do. Think, Jaiden!

Okay, she was right. But it's been a while...

"Yes! There's a little stream nearby. Hear it? I can't remember if the clearing is up or downstream, but I recall a little open space. Not much. I hope I can remember which way to turn."

Let's go!

I listened carefully, heard the distant whisper of the stream and we headed for it.

I was afraid I would outrun the lumbering beast behind me, but she nearly ran over me a couple of times as I paused to get my bearings. The gurgle of the water became a whoosh, then a much louder hiss, and finally a thundering roar.

We came into a sunlit spot revealing a five-foot high waterfall. Here was a small clearing.

"What are you going to do?" I said.

I'm flying out of here. I'm still tired and sore, but with those hounds and the railroad men close behind, I'll find the strength. But what can you do?

"Don't worry about me, just go, now!" I shouted above the roar.

Before I can fly higher than a few feet above the tracks like when I tow the train, I need you to loosen the hobble that restricts the reach of my wings.

Skye hunkered so I could loosen the straps that held her wings close to her body. Removing the bolts and rings, the wide net of straps fell on both sides of her body.

Good. Step back, quickly!

I did but I didn't take my eyes off her. This was going to be good!

She looked up, and moved her head back and forth. Was she gauging the distance and angle of flight? I guess. Who knows? I don't fly.

With a grunt, she reached the tips of her wings above her head, and pulled down both wings keeping them from hitting the trees that closed in on her. She soared upward about three feet, then hung suspended for a moment before she sank to the ground. She reached high and flapped her wings again, so fast it didn't look physically possible.

Her body rose again, several more feet this time. Then she stretched her neck and tail and as she quickly stroked her wings again, she tilted back with her tail touching the ground and pushed off to soar above the treetops.

Free of the surrounding trees, she spread her wings wide and in two mighty flaps, she disappeared from sight. The branches and leaves swayed and broke off as if from a hurricane force wind and blew me backward onto my bottom.

Just as the dust from the dragon's launch settled, a pack of baying hounds and five yelling and cursing men close behind burst into the clearing.

Dogs and men looked skyward. Two of the men swung their crossbows up and fired arrows or bolts, as they called them, that arched toward the space Skye had just occupied before disappearing. The bolts sliced through the trees hitting nothing but branches and leaves.

"Which way is that monster headed, boy?" the lead man bellowed. "Some old coot in town said you went into the forest with a horse as big as a dragon!" He laughed, but a snarl quickly replaced his smile. "You better answer true because we have no patience with dragon thieves,"

He motioned to guy behind him to come to me. "Clod, get up here."

I looked up. This Clod was bigger than anyone I knew. And, to me, he looked *mean*.

"I don't know," I said. "She didn't tell me. Do you think dragons can talk?" Oops, I said too much, but it was too late.

"Of course not, you idiot!" the lead man said. "But I think you know which way it went—"

"No, I don't because you and your dogs made such a racket and busted in here scaring me to death. I have no idea where it went. This forest is big and there's thousands of places it could have gone. How am I supposed to know? I don't even know these woods—"

"Shut up, punk," Clod said. "Who asked for your comments?"

I started to give him a smart remark, but then realized this guy was far meaner than my father. Dad was strict but he wasn't mean-hearted. He just lost patience with me, sometimes.

Clod kicked at me and raised his hand to knock the stuffing out of me, but the boss grabbed his hand. "No, don't waste your strength. He's just a kid. How's he supposed to know where the dragon's going?"

The boss turned to me. "Right, kid?"

"Yeah, right. She forced me to take her into the forest—" Oops, again. Saying too much.

"Now how do you know it's a female and how could a sick dragon force you to do something like that?"

Think. Think!

"I call almost every big animal 'she' because most everything on my Dad's farm is female. All the cows except for our one lazy bull. All the chickens except for our stupid rooster. And the horses? Well one's female the other male. I did have a boy dog, but he went missing over a year ago. I never thought about it with the dragon, just called it she."

I think I was talking too much, but the boss seemed satisfied with my answer. I have no idea how I was able to think that fast because I actually thought about the dragon as an 'it' until she made it clear she was female.

"Okay, Mr. Smart Guy," he said, "so what about the dragon forcing you to take it away from the train station?"

That was easy. "Truth is, it or she is so big and I've never been close to a dragon before. Only saw them pass by town from a distance. Once I got into town, I still was a little ways away, so up close, I was scared and never thought about it being sick or anything. I mean, that thing's wing could crush me with one flap! And it's got long teeth, a hot breath—"

"Well, kid, I guess it doesn't matter because here you are. And out there," he motioned to the sky and forest surrounding us, "is where the dragon is. Blast it!" He turned to the four other men, "I guess we go back to town and send a message to Portville that we've lost the dragon and we'll need some gold and silver dragons to find it. Here I thought we were coming to pick up a dead one."

He grabbed my shoulder, turned me around and pushed me ahead of the other men. "Back to town, punk."

In all the commotion, especially the appearance of these scary men, I had forgotten I had my knife and sling. I didn't dare reach for them right at that moment or at all because these guys could flatten me before I could pull anything out of my pouch. I just hoped they wouldn't discover what I had and take them away from me.

Anyway, I wasn't entirely sure of myself leading the way, so I kept my eyes on the path, bypassing side trails that didn't look well-traveled. Scared I would make a mistake and get beaten, I decided to express occasional doubt out loud.

"I think it's this way, though it's hard to tell, never been in this part of the forest before."

"Yeah, well maybe, maybe not. You get us lost and your rear end gets kicked between your ears. Got it?"

"Got it."

So much for trying to avoid getting punished for making a mistake.

We approached the stream. Had the dragon and I come this way a little while ago? The forest looked familiar on the other side of the stream, so maybe—
Don't turn your head, Jaiden. Stay focused in front of you, and don't say anything.
Was this the dragon's voice in my head? But I heard it so clearly. I started to comment.
Quiet, I said! You say anything in front of these brutes and both of us are dead meat.
Yes, it was Skye. So, she was in my head because a sideways look at one of the men close to me showed someone just ambling along without a thought.
Now what? Do I do something or think—
No need, the voice said in my head. *I don't exactly read thoughts but when you want to say something, I can hear it in my head.*
Oh, that's creepy.
Sorry. Don't worry. If you wish to think something privately, I can't hear it.
So, you say, but how do I know?
You don't, but that's not important. I'm nearby and I'm going to try to get you away from these men before things get really ugly.
For me or for you?
Both. How happy is your father going to be when you get back to Hilltop?
Okay, you made your point. Where are you?
To your left—don't look! These people aren't used to being in a deep forest, so even I can blend in pretty well unless they really look hard to see me.
Now what?

I'm now standing in the stream so you'll be able to run downstream and find me. Break away fast enough, so they'll have to chase you. When they come around the bend, I'll do my dragon thing and put the fear of death in them.

You think they're afraid of you? They're used to dealing with dragons.

Only when they're harnessed, chained, and staked down. And that's after shooting us with a weak poison to bring us to our knees. They aren't prepared to meet me because in the heat of the chase, some of them must have left their crossbows back on the trail somewhere. Only two of them fired at me.

How did you know that? I thought. You were gone before they fired.

I have eyesight better than you realize and I was high enough above the trees, I saw two very sharp bolts arch over the trees.

The other three must have had too much gear to carry while they were trying to catch us, I thought. Anyway, I think we're coming back a different way, so we must have already passed by their weapons. We don't have much time because I'll bet, they're getting anxious to get their weapons back in their hands.

Skye may have not been the only one to read my mind because the leader said, "Wait up. Where is our gear? We couldn't have left it behind this far?"

He stepped forward, grabbed my shoulder and slung me around. "What game are you playing, punk?"

"No game! I didn't know you had gear! I'm trying the best I can to stay on the trail—"

"Shut up," he said. He slapped me so hard, I saw flashing candles. "Let's go back to where we started and try again. And if we don't find the dragon...."

I couldn't let this go on. I was within inches of stepping on the first stone to cross the stream. I had to run down the stream if I wanted a chance to escape.

I tried an old trick as I looked to my far right and shouted, "There she is! She's going to kill us all."

The two with weapons raised them ready to fire, while the others scrambled to gather rocks and sticks as they stared hard up the stream, the wrong way.

I spun and ducked to break the leader's grip on me but he held tight. I ended by spinning right into the water and pulling the man on top of me.

I flailed wildly to get him off and get out of his grip. Didn't work. "Hey, you idiots," he yelled. "He's playing games! Get back here!"

But the others didn't listen as they tried to cross the stream while keeping their eyes peeled for the sight of the dragon upstream.

The leader let loose with some words I only heard Dad use when he was really, really mad. I rolled from under him though still in his grip. Then a screech sounded behind me as if from the very depths of Hades as it tore through the trees and echoed in all directions. The men froze and turned downstream.

There was the dragon straddling the water.

FOUR

Hang On!

That was what I needed. I left my captor with a piece of my shirt in his hand as I ran toward the great beast. I nearly caught my feet in between rocks in the stream but kept upright as I reached my rescuer.

Skye's swift pivot away from me seemed impossible for one of such bulk and height. I heard the whiz of bolts fly only inches away from my head. I saw one graze the back of her neck, but it merely bounced off.

We both tore down the stream around a sharp bend. Beyond the sight of the men, the dragon leaned down, nose to nose with me.

You have to climb on me and hang on to my harness like your life depended on it because it will. We're going to fly.

I had nothing to say. I must have looked like a stupid mule.

Now! If they reach us, you're done for!

I scanned the harness made of wide, thick leather that wrapped between the base of the big reptile's neck and her wings. That was one huge piece of leather.

No matter. I reached up, gripped the harness just below the attached saddle bag and pulled myself up the side of the dragon.

Not all the way to the top, she said. *The wind will blow you off even if you don't get dizzy and fall off. Stay right where you are. Make sure your hands and your feet are jammed tight between the harness and my hide. Grip both straps around my neck and shoulders. Plaster yourself against me or the wind will rip you away from me.*

"Okay! Okay! I'm going to die!" But I did as she said.

Probably so, but it's our only chance. Ready, Jaiden?

"No, but go ahead, Skye, let's get out of here!"

We both heard the angry cries and churning water as the men came around the bend.

They roared a terrifying battle howl that froze my blood.

The dragon spread her wings like the broadest branches of an ancient oak tree. The wing tips rose high and slapped down in a blur. And again. And again. I felt the pit of my stomach push into my bowels. I started to throw up as we became airborne.

I sure hoped the wind from her wings blew off more bolts sure to come our way.

Lucky me, we rose so fast, the contents of my stomach couldn't push hard enough to reach my mouth. I hugged Skye's body tighter than anything or anyone I ever held. To the left I saw the tops of the trees disappear downward.

The blue of the sky and scattered clouds was all I could see. I turned to face the scaly hide of the dragon and pressed the sweaty harness to my face. I couldn't breathe, preventing cries of terror from escaping my lips.

Now my stomach and my whole body felt light as if I were falling, but I knew I wasn't. I clenched my eyes closed so tightly I saw red and white streaks behind my eyelids.

The low whirring tones of the dragon's wings filled my ears as her body rocked slightly, the each beat of her wings kept us from falling out of the sky.

Then the rocking stopped. I forced one eye open. We were still high above the forest. Distant green fields were almost lost in a mist. The great wings were outstretched as we glided.

The forest swept away under us revealing a dark green meadow below. A rocky ridge bordered the meadow. We angled sharply downward. I panicked.

We were falling! I started to black out. But I struggled to tighten my hands' grip on the harness. I still felt the scaly hide, smelled the leather.

A sharp jolt and a couple of shifts of Skye's body to the left, then the right and then…

The sensation of no longer moving. We were down. I was still alive!

When I tried to open my eyes, the whole world disappeared. I felt myself lose consciousness.

FIVE

The Cave of the Dragon

I had never been on a mountain and especially in a cave. I once climbed to the top of the highest hill behind our farm. Now I viewed that distant hill from the ridge where the dragon landed. It was quite a sight. The whole Emerald Forest spread before me like a giant pasture. Beyond that was the valley where Hilltop sat but it wasn't visible from here, only the hills behind our farm were visible.

I might have seen our farm but I needed the vision of an eagle or, perhaps, a dragon. I had never been so far away from home, either. Not ever. It felt strange like I was missing something inside which made me anxious to go back home.

Even with a very angry Dad waiting for me.

Heavy footsteps behind me. I turned and said, "Is this where you once lived?" I motioned toward the cave several steps behind us.

No, but it's not far from here. Far away from people, their farms, towns, and big barns where they broke our spirits and strapped on the harnesses that kept us under control.

"How is that possible? You're so big and powerful. Why you're five times bigger than our biggest bull. And you can fly!"

True, but people are cunning. Far more powerful than their bodies. That's where we made our mistake. Small bands of people ventured into our lands, climbed to our caves.

"Just like that?"

Oh no, there were wars. We burned many human armies and their encampments. But some figured how to track us back to our caves and then how to overpower us. I don't want to talk about it now, but tonight I will tell my story.

"Okay." I was both fascinated and terrified to think about how such magnificent beasts could be brought down and used as war and train machines. I had no idea how long ago people defeated the dragons, so I was anxious to hear the story.

As the sun was setting, I searched for wild versions of food we had on the farm: groundnuts which are somewhat like potatoes, wild corn, pine nuts, greens. I had hoped for a little meat like a squirrel or doves I could bring down with my sling and dress with my knife, but none of those beasts made their presence known, so we had to make do with the vegetables.

As darkness descended, with no means to cook, and the dragon unable to produce her own fire to cook for me, I ate the food raw as we sat in the dark cavern. Not very tasty, a little bitter, except the corn which was as sweet as our own but the cobs very tiny. I noticed the dragon ate only the corn. I should have gathered way more corn but... oh well!

"So, what should I call you? I'm Jaiden," I said.

When she looked deep into my eyes earlier, it had scared me, but now it no longer bothered me. It seemed to be the way she tested my honesty and intentions.

I was called Skye because my color matched the sky better than my nest mates. Now, I'm only Number 4.

"I like Skye. In Hilltop we all have plain names that don't mean anything and aren't interesting."

"Hmmm."

I smiled at the sound she made deep in her throat. Reminded me of my father's grumbling which always made me chuckle inside. "So… what about your story?"

Ah, yes, the story.

She raised her head and looked out the mouth of the cave and studied the stars.

I don't know where to start because the early wars were before my time. I was a child of ten winters when all the dragons were finally defeated. But I remember my father's stories.

Dark Cloud was his name. He was our clan's story teller so the stories are quite dramatic. I was to be the next storyteller so he trained me and repeated the stories over and over so I could learn them as he had from his mother.

Now there are different kinds of dragons. I should tell you about those before I tell my father's story. The silver battle dragons could easily handle groups of nearly a hundred human soldiers while the small gold dragons flew low and got the drop on many small clusters of men—

"Wait a minute, I've never seen silver or gold dragons," I said. "All I've heard are some things that sound like fairy tales because the so-called facts keep changing. In one story the silver dragons are demons who bite people and infect them with their poison. And they're bigger than blue dragons and can burn a whole village in one breath...."

Hmm, I see what you mean, Jaiden. People tend to make up a lot of stupid tales without even knowing. Silver dragons are smaller than me. Perhaps the size of one of your large horses but longer and thinner, shaped like a lizard.

Their size allowed them to fly fast, knock down trees when humans hide under them, and burn, at close range, almost a dozen soldiers in battle. Big enough, yet not too big. Each blue one like me could burn hundreds in one pass from several yards away, but we couldn't protect ourselves too well. The silver and gold dragons escorted us to provide protection.

Where a silver dragon can shift and turn quicker than us blues, the golds are about the size of big dog and skinny like a snake. They fly in packs and could take on one, maybe two soldiers at a time. They breathed fire, but it'll only scorch a person. It's their bite. It's poisonous. They're the only dragons that are venomous.

"Wow, I like that," I said. "Well... I mean not for our soldiers but to be able to fly, burn, and bite like that. How could people defeat all of you?"

The early battles were easily won by the dragons as dozens would attack the human soldiers from all directions. We blues could have dropped boulders on them, but it was more effective to cover them in fire. Since we can only shoot the fire from our mouths, we have to fly low and slow. A few of us were killed by their arrows and spears if they hit our tender stomachs, but it took far more than one arrow or spear.

For years the soldiers came and went during the seasons for battle—spring and summer. Then we didn't see them for over a generation. But something changed. They had developed more deadly weapons like crossbows and cannons. More of us died. We couldn't fly so low. And even the silvers and golds could be picked off more often than not.

We resorted to luring them to our mountains and sending massive land and rock slides on their heads. Worked for a while.

Finally, a year or so after my grandfather and grandmother were betrothed, their oldest child, my father, and his younger brothers and sisters were born. The humans finally found our caves when my father was grown but they could not bring their heavy weapons up the steep cliffs without being seen. So, dragons thought they were safe. But....

"What happened? Were all dragons in danger, even the silver and gold dragons, too?" I asked.

It was probably the same for all kinds of dragons, Jaiden. I do know that once the humans gained control of the gold and silver dragons, they limited their abilities to spit fire.

This is what my father, Dark Cloud, told me about how it happened to blue dragons like him when he was only a youngster....

SIX

Dark Cloud's Tale

Dark Cloud said:
One night, Mother fixed a meal of thistle and rabbit, my favorite. We had no shortage of animals living in our cave because it was warm during cold nights and there were always our left-over bones and scraps these beasts could eat. Lucky for them, some of those animals weren't tasty to us, such as wolves.

Father, why do we let these little furry beasts live among us? I asked. *They seem kind of grouchy always growling at each other and us if we get too near them."*

Dark Cloud, Father said to me. *They aren't very friendly, but they are good hunting partners, sniffing prey, and they bark if strangers are near.*

Well, I guess that was okay, but one day, all our wolves disappeared.

My mother said, *This worries me. They have always been around. The little black female was friendly with me and now I miss her.*

Father went for a short flight circling our caves, following some of the canyon trails the wolves usually traveled for hunting. But he came back alone and thoughtful.

It is strange because they always went up and down canyons yet I didn't catch sight of them today. They had dens for their pups during birthing season. They never allowed pups to come to the caves until they were fullgrown, yet they were usually nearby. Those dens are empty now which isn't right this time of year.

They probably lost their pups, Mother said.

Both Father and Mother were so disturbed that none of us youngsters spoke about it then. Later, when we did, they ignored us and talked about other things.

Then in a couple of months, the wolves were back!

But they weren't the same. They smelled the same, but they were fatter and very awkward. They could hardly walk across a rocky slope without falling and getting their feet caught between rocks. Still they hung around the caves and took our dinner scraps to eat.

Mother said, *Even though they stay farther away from us around the cave, they are always watching me and the youngsters. They don't go off anymore. They're always underfoot. Very strange.*

I know, Father said. *But they are an odd breed. Smart in their own ways, but not like us. They used to make noises among themselves like whining, grunting, barking, and growling. But they didn't talk like us. I didn't think they knew how, but lately I've heard them make sounds almost like talking.*

I interrupted and said, *Well, I was a little closer to them last night and I swear they were talking but it wasn't in the dragon tongue. It wasn't wolf noises either. They just aren't the same and I don't like them anymore.*

After giving me a hard look for interrupting him, Father said, *Let's be patient. Something bad has happened to them. I'm sure losing all their pups has something to do with it. So, we have to understand and not fuss too much about it.*

Mother wasn't so sure. *I just don't like how they have been acting lately. And there are things missing from my supplies. Some of our minerals and cooking oil. Why would those disappear?*

Father chuckled and turned to me. *Dark Cloud, wolves don't have any need for our minerals because they don't spout fire and they certainly don't cook.* He laughed a little harder which encouraged me and my younger brothers and sisters to join in.

Mother only grimaced.

This was one of the few times I ever knew my father to be wrong about something, though I didn't say it.

The next night, it was past dark before only two wolves came in. Where were they rest of them? They slunk to their usual sleeping spots and curled up without checking around the fire pit for dinner scraps.

After a few minutes we all gathered around the fire, Father telling stories of his grandfather the great warrior. One of the wolves howled in a funny voice that sounded very different from their usual barks and howls.

All of a sudden, a swarm of beasts came into our caves. The beasts were small and stood upright—humans! Human warriors. They began throwing spears with ropes tied to them. The spears pierced our legs, tails, and more importantly, our wings.

The spears hurt but they weren't deadly. Much more painful than damaging. We fought back but the humans danced around the rocks and hid. Ten at a time would jump out to throw spears and then scurry around to avoid capture. We did get ahold of a few in our mouths and slammed them against the walls.

We could have flown away if we had been in the open, but in the small space of our caves we couldn't take flight.

Many spear-points dug in to our skin so deeply we couldn't rip them out. The men pulled on the ropes and ran around us tightening the ropes causing more pain. We could hardly move. But we thought it would be all over when my parents drew in deep breaths and exhaled, trying to burn the little men like rabbits on a stick. Nothing came out of their mouths except wheezing breath.

What was this?

Again, and again, they drew in huge volumes of air and blew out—nothing but weaker and weaker breaths. How did they lose their fire?

To make it worse, I was too young to have a tough fire-pouch in the lower part of my neck above my shoulder blades, so I couldn't blow fire onto an enemy.

The men began dancing as we weakened and the ropes tightened so that we couldn't budge.

They made awful hooting, cackling, and whooping sounds. I think they were saying words, but it sounded very savage to me.

We were captured!

My father wailed and shrieked in a way I never heard from a dragon, a mixture of anger and grief. He had failed to defend his family against these beastly humans. He feared his family would all die and be butchered like rodents.

That didn't happen, but we were carried off on big wagons and put in a smelly, cold corral as if we were the human's cows and horses. Like animals!

That was the beginning of the end of dragon freedom. Without our fire and unable to get near them with their spears, whips, and crossbows, we had lost the war.

They made us beasts of burden and weapons in their stupid wars among themselves. They held our children captive and tortured us with their weapons, forcing us to help them bring down our own kind as they worked their way through our mountain caverns defeating all but a few who fought and clawed their way to escape.

Those escapees were never heard from again.

My family was sad beyond belief. How could this have happened to blue dragons who were so strong and their flame so hot and deadly? Yet it did.

And there's nothing more to be said.

SEVEN

A Little Dragon Chemistry

A long silence grew between Skye and me. Hanging my head in shame, I watched Skye stare at the ground, her breathing labored like a dying horse.

How could my people do that to such wonderful beasts? In fact, I couldn't think of the dragons as beasts anymore. I think we're the beasts.

"I don't know what to say." As I looked at the big blue dragon, I realized she couldn't reply either. But I had to say something.

"I wouldn't do that to you or your kind," I said. "I never thought about it. Maybe I thought you were big dumb beasts like our farm animals and you didn't mind pulling trains and fighting in battles for us."

An offended look swept across her face, but I couldn't stop myself from continuing. "Why couldn't your father and his parents use their flames? Your story of fire-breathing dragons sounds like others I've heard, though I thought they were all fairy tales, boogey men or stupid things like that."

Her look softened a little, as much as a huge dragon face could soften. *It's the minerals Father mentioned in his story. It's how we can ignite and spew the flames, Jaiden*

"Minerals, huh? What kind?"

Well, some yellowish gravel and burned wood. When we finish burning wood for a meal or to keep warm, we collect the blackened wood and swallow it and the gravel, not into our stomachs, but into our fire-pouches. Something happens in there and it gets very hot. When we burp, the gas and gravel—I think your people call it sulfur—flares up.

I was stunned. Who would have guessed? I thought it was some magical power.

"So, your breath, yellow gravel and the wood make the heat in your, uh, fire-pouches?"

Don't know for sure. I think that's why we have the pouches to start with, to collect this vile gas instead of burping it all the way out. When the heat increases in our pouches, we can easily release whatever brews in our pouch."

It made sense because when my father wanted to grill or dry big slabs of meat, he used charcoal or burned wood, as Skye called it, to create a long-lasting, hot source to cook the meats.

"So, what happened to your grandparents' yellow gravel? Why couldn't they burn the humans dressed in wolves clothing?" I smirked a little thinking about how that twisted the common saying of "wolves dressed in sheep's clothing."

Skye answered. *They stole my grandparent's sulfur and replaced it with yellow-colored sand, soaked all the dragon's charcoal in water, and returned it to the firepit when the outside was dry, but the charcoal was too wet inside and it couldn't spark into flame.*

"Well, now, there you are," I said. "But I don't quite understand how what comes from your pouches makes flames in the first place."

Skye laughed. *That I can explain. When our fire-pouches grow tough enough to withstand the heat from the sulfur, charcoal and stomach gas, we gather pieces of flint.*

"Like what people make arrowheads with?"

Yes. She leaned near my face and opened her big mouth. For a moment I thought I was going to be her evening snack. But I couldn't resist examining her rows of teeth in the upper and lower jaws. They were magnificent. Long, sharp, some even hooked slightly to make it impossible for prey to get loose.

To my relief she slowly closed her mouth.

Jaiden, did you notice the gaps between my front teeth?

"Sort of. You kind of scared me. For a moment there, I thought you were going—"

—to eat you? She smiled. *"I am rather hungry, but not for young men. My point—,* she chuckled in a weird grunting way, *—is that those gaps make it possible for us to jam pieces of flint between our front teeth, both our uppers and lowers.*

"Okay… and?"

When we burp the gases from our pouch, we grind our front teeth sharply to make a small spark which causes the gas to burn. We exhale a big breath and fry a few puny humans. Sorry, no offense, you're not puny.

"Oh." Still it was a scary thought to think about that fire coming from her mouth. Luckily, I remembered she said her pouch was empty and I didn't see any flint between her teeth.

You're relieved, of course, she said. *I wouldn't burn my new little human friend, but I would gladly incinerate my captors and handlers who enjoy cruelty. But I'm not here to find sulfur and stick flint between my teeth. Though that may not be such a bad idea.*

She paused a moment, looking at me as if wondering what I would do next. I forced myself to remain calm and merely looked at her as pleasantly as I could manage.

I only want to return to my cave home, maybe find fellow clanspeople, even a brother or sister who escaped or never was captured. I want to live a normal dragon life.

"So, you think it's possible you have family living free?"

That's another story.

"Well, the night is young and I'm not tired yet. What happened to you? If your father was captured when he was a, uh, child, what about you?"

Father grew up in the dragon stockades and over the years his father and mother were taken away never to be seen again. Then his brothers and sisters were taken. He was put in a corral with other blue dragons about his same age. But as he grew older, they were separated into separate barns because the humans feared what they could do if two or more of the males were kept together.

It was around about then he met my mother....

"Oh. Then all your family lived in captivity."

Not exactly. Let me continue his story.

EIGHT

Dark Cloud's Family on the Farm

D ark Cloud said:
I was bored during those early days after we were captured. Now that the humans had us, they didn't know what to do with us.

My father said, *I fear we won't have long. Why would they want to feed us for no reason?"*

Mother got angry. *Shush! Do you want to scare the children! You don't know what they have in mind.*

No, I don't but I don't think we're going to become circus animals trained to do stupid tricks and carry humans around wearing ugly costumes.

Circus? Costumes? What are those? Mother asked.

When I wandered about as a youngster, I watched these circus things from a distance. It's a show where people watch animals do dumb things for fun. They even put human-like clothing on them. People feel superior to see animals act that way. Believe me, they don't trust us enough to think we would be safe in a big tent with lots of gawking people looking at us. And who thinks we would do tricks, anyway?

No more, she said. Father obeyed though he made it clear he didn't like to be ordered around in front of the children. The whole thing was humiliating without fighting a losing battle with his wife.

At the time, I didn't understand what my father and mother were upset about. I just thought they would make us pull wagons and plows. I saw cows and horses working on the farm on the other side of the fence that surrounded the place where they kept us. Why put us on a farm if they weren't going to use us as farm animals?

My thought was confirmed when, as the weather began to warm up, they brought huge wagons into our corrals. Carpenters brought large poles, cutting and fitting them to the wagons. Soon they were fitting long wide leather straps around my father and mother. That wasn't easy for the wary carpenters.

Of course, they feared my parents would thrash around swinging their long tails and flapping their huge but clipped wings whenever the men got near. But they shouldn't have feared because on the nights before the carpenters came to the dragon pens, they fed us some strange mash with our slop of pork, beef, and groundnuts. It tasted good but we all got really sleepy well before our usual time to settle down to sleep.

The next morning, we all felt so tired and woozy that we didn't mild the human handlers leading us to the carpenters while we stood—barely—as they fitted the poles and leather straps to us so we could tow the wagons. It was at that point we realized our wings were not only clipped but strapped against our backs. They had made big halters that made it impossible to flap them to fly or hurt our handlers.

From then on, we were fed the mash as they trained us to pull the wagons and take direction from the handlers. We were never tied up like when they first captured us because the halters allowed us to be controlled.

So that was our life for a few years. Working the farms pulling wagons five to ten times bigger than the those they used before. Soon they had us plowing fields, walking in circles to run their threshing machines and even their mills if the farm wasn't near a stream for water power.

As my siblings grew and became more powerful and trained to these different tasks, my parents were taken away. Did they simply take them to other large farms or were they killed and butchered? We saw what they did to the cattle and pigs, why not us once we got too old to labor in the fields?

I didn't want to think about my parents as slabs of meat hanging in a cold cellar, and I certainly didn't share my thoughts with my younger brothers and sisters. I hoped they were still too young to think of such things when they, too, were taken away, one at a time for the next few years. I hope they ended up working at other farms.

Now I was alone.

One bright summer morning, I heard the sound of a dragon stirring in the barn next to mine. More captives? I went into the corral and sniffed the air. I grunted in such a low tone, the humans wouldn't be able to overhear—a trick my father taught me before he was taken away.

"Hmm."

No response.

"Hmm," I said again.

Maybe this was just a thing only my father did as a way to communicate to my mother and us youngsters?

Then, a little bit thinner grunt but still below human hearing, "Hmm?"

Well, maybe it wasn't just my father's trick.

"Hmm-hmm," I replied.

"Hmmmm," came the longer response with the pitch sliding higher almost within human perception.

Right at that point, a farm boy came out of the barn next to mine lugging a wagon with a water barrel strapped to it. He calmly filled the trough, looked at me with vacant eyes, and then disappeared back into the barn.

I heard heavy-footed rustling about in the second barn over. Then here came the slimmest, most beautiful blue dragon I had ever seen. A sweet scent like wildflowers drifted my way and I almost swooned and fell. This was stronger than the strange mash. I might not have had the gumption to do any work that day if I inhaled any more of that tangy perfume.

Since the only female blues I knew were my mother and my two little sisters, it took a few moments to realize this was another one. But she was nothing like the females I knew. In spite of my woozy head, I felt energized. I wanted to rear up on my back legs and take flight, roar with joy, and incinerate every barn on the whole farm.

Of course, I couldn't. But I felt like it!

Hello, a soft voice said.

I swung my head around not knowing that sweet voice came from the new female across the fences. I heard laughter. My neck stretched toward the double row of barriers between us and tried to reach into her corral. Nope, not quite. Our corrals were too far apart to allow such an indiscretion.

Was that you? I said, sounding more idiotic than my goofy little brother.

Who else? She smiled in that secret way only other dragons can see.

Excuse me, but it's been a while since I've seen or heard a fellow, or... lady dragon since my parents and siblings were taken away years ago. What brings you here to this farm?

A big old wagon pulled by some big old blue like you, though it wasn't you, she said.

No, I would have remembered that. I haven't been off this farm since we were captured years ago at the end of the wars. I grew up here. Once my family was gone, I thought I was all they needed for dragon duty. But... I guess not.

Have you been happier alone?

Oh no, not at— I realized I was starting to sound a little pathetic, maybe even desperate. After all, I was past the age for First Mating. Back when my father patiently explained to me the ways of adults, mating and having a family I would day-dream endlessly.

Tamping down those thoughts, I watched her reaction to me. She didn't seem amused, though there was a sparkle in her eye that I had never seen in a blue before. Was that what a female did when she saw her mate for the first time?

She lowered her head and examined the hay at her feet. But she didn't eat it. Was she sparing me embarrassment? Surely, she was experienced in the ways of mating. In fact, at that moment I suddenly swung my neck toward her barn, sniffed and listened intently.

Did she come with her mate? She didn't say anything about coming with someone else, but—

What are you looking for?" she said with a dragon chuckle. Such a tender chuckle.

Uhm, I don't— Well, I wondered if there were others who came with you?

No. Just me. I think they brought me for you. No one told me that, but now that I see you and... that look in your eyes, and the scent you're giving off.

Oh, Lord of the Dragons, am I that obvious? That pathetic!

But she only smiled as if seeing a delicate butterfly land on her nose. She then pivoted, walked to the trough, and took her time getting a drink of water. I watched in fascination as if I had never seen a female drink water.

She lifted her head, looked at me sideways and sauntered back into the barn.

Oh. Gone so soon? Is she totally bored with me? Will she be taken away now that she has rejected her assigned mate? What do those stupid, mean humans know anyway?

Actually, they know a lot. I was completely taken by her. Though I didn't know her name, her scent would never leave my memory, even if they had taken her away forever that very same day.

I had no idea what to do. I waited in my corral staring at her doorway. Nothing. Not the sound of her shuffling around inside or laying down for a nap.

Finally, one of my idiot handlers came out, yakking and snorting like some demented raccoon while he strapped on my harness and led me out for a day of cultivating the north section. Weeds wait for no man or dragon.

The day went by in a daze. I pulled my cultivator, ate my oats and chicken scraps, but had no conscious connection to the world or even the soil beneath my feet. I only forgot the funky fog as I ate my dinner in my trough outside the barn.

I took one look toward the doorway of the second barn. Then I started in to try to find a way to go to sleep. When I stepped in the barn, I heard a breezy sigh.

I peeked back out the barn door. Only a few feet away was that beautiful blue face looking at me. Smiling at me.

Had a hard day in the fields? she said.
I wouldn't know. I was in a daze— Dragon God, again! I said what I thought instead of something intelligent or at least not so obvious. *I didn't feel so good today.* Oh, that's certainly better! Shut up, you clueless idiot! The farm boy has you all beat in brains today!
Me, too, she said simply. *You made a big impression on me. I really expected some big old guy somewhat past it in age or manliness. Or, maybe, some boy without any class,* she winked at me.
Winked!
I guess I'm the second choice. 'Some boy.'
She gave a hearty laugh. *Yes, that's it!*
I couldn't keep my head from sinking to the ground. I watched the dust swirl around as my nostrils blew big puffs of frustration out.
No, she added more quietly. *I'm kidding. My mother told me to not be such a kidder, but that's just me.* There was a long pause. I mustered the energy to lift my head a little to dare look at her.
She smiled that smile again. *I'm really impressed with you. You're much better than I expected. And if I get to know you more—maybe you're even better than I could have hoped for. What do you think?*
That was it! I couldn't blow this now. I tried to slowly raise my head and keep a calm expression on my face. I merely nodded my head and pointed to the far end of our corrals with my chin.
You want to go to the fence and watch the sun set? I think we need to get better acquainted. By the way, my name is Dark Cloud.

She nodded slightly and answered, *Call me Springwind.* We strolled to the end of our respective corrals. I don't know where the things that came out of my brain while we talked that evening, but it was wonderful. The freshness of the first time with the one you are to love for the rest of your life was so overwhelming I almost swooned and fainted right in front of her.

But the Dragon God was with me and I came off pretty good, at least that's what she told me many times for years after that. Soon, our handlers saw their calculation about our mating was spot-on and she was brought into my barn where we lived together and gave birth to you and your brothers and sisters until the Medial Wars.

Yes, the Medials when the dragons tried to take back their freedom for once and for all. Just before that time, I grew anxious. It was one thing for your mother and I to tow farm wagons around, but to think they would soon train our children to do the same as they grew larger... that broke our hearts. We were old enough to remember freedom, but this wasn't the fate of our children, not if I died trying.

For years, we both watched how things were done around the farm. Where the people spent their time, what their routines were, and how careful or careless they could be. And the farm itself. Were there any places where we might escape if given the chance? Neither of us could stand to leave without the other. And then, with children, we had to figure how it could be done so all of us could escape at the same time.

In the middle of the deep, dark days of winter, they had a celebration welcoming the point when the days grew longer again. That celebration called for lots of drinking and eating. But better yet, it meant no one wanted to miss the fun. And they were certainly prone to stumbling around, drunk on their beer and wine, ready to carouse through the night and sleep away what was left of the night and the next morning.

Your mother and I knew we couldn't wait until the next year or two to make our move. Already, you, Skye, were old enough for training when Spring came. Though your siblings were years away from that maturity, we had to take the chance.

It was a cold snowy night. The wind blew hard, freezing man and dragon to the bone. My handler and I returned hauling enough wood in a big sled for their celebration and for their stoves until the next afternoon. I was done for the day. As I returned from the forest that bordered the farm, I watched my handler carefully.

He had been drinking beer since noon. So, when he opened the gate to the barnyard and came along my side to guide me through, I kept going toward the wood shed without stopping for him to close the gate behind.

"Hey, stupid lizard, slow down, I can't close the—" he said. But the harder he pulled on the reins, the more I plodded on groaning as if in pain from the freezing wind.

Then he said, "Aw, hell with it, I'll get the gate later."

After I helped unload the bigger logs, he strayed a little too close to me. I nudged him slightly and he lost his footing and fell in a pile of old dragon dung.

"Dad-blamed, overgrown lizard! I ought to slam you! This is a pile of your brains, you're so stupid! Now I gotta go wash up before the party."

He man-handled me, whipped my buttocks a couple of times, but by the weakness of his blows I could tell he was very drunk. In fact, he almost fell face-first in the hay underneath my feet. I could have crushed him, but that was too risky if he screamed and brought others.

I let him get away with that foolish mistake. He stood again and tried to brush off the hay. I slowly moved toward the part of the shed where they stored the big sled. He staggered onto his feet and shuffled along behind me. He unhitched me and took me out the door and to our barn. He even forgot to close the shed door behind him as he tried to stay with me.

Another mistake. I could have crushed him, released my family and escaped but we wouldn't have gone more than a few hundred yards before the whole farm and their dogs would have been hot on our trail. I slowed and waited patiently as he came around, unlocked our barn door and whipped my sides to get me in. He latched the door behind him, but that was all right because he had neglected to close and lock the gate from the fields.

Over the last several weeks before that night, our whole family had pushed and pulled on the vertical logs that formed the walls of our barn, especially those that held the hinges of the massive door. Every night we pushed and moved those logs. At first it seemed we didn't budge them. But eventually they started to wiggle a little in their deep holes. We always made sure the hay and dirt around their bases was pushed against the logs and patted down so no man could see they were no longer tightly secured in the hard ground.

On this night of the human celebration, it took very little effort for us to loosen them to the point they fell over, taking the heavy door with them. Your mother had already packed hay and that horrid meal that passed for dragon food in several cast-off gunny sacks. As you remember, you children each took one or two of the sacks in your mouths and we set out.

I went first and crept near the long bunkhouse where the celebration was in full swing. People, music, laughing, yelling, and all sorts of racket made it clear to me that the party was rolling and nothing short of a volcano could have distracted their attention.

Perfect.

I went back to your mother and all you young ones huddled in a tight circle braving the vicious wind.

This is it. Let's go. Quickly. I'll follow behind in case someone sees us leaving. It will be miserable across the fields, but you'll hardly feel the wind among the trees. From there, you'll follow me. I've tramped all over that dense forest helping gather firewood and know a way out. Beyond the far ridges are more patches of forest where we can rest. But we can't stop for long until we've left this valley.

Go! Go! Go! Springwind, my mate, my love called, and so her and you children rushed ahead of me.

Through the gate and across the field. I looked back and my heart sank. There was someone walking along the barn nearest the gate. They reached to steady themselves against the barn. I saw them struggle to unbutton their pants.

A call of nature. But he turned to see the gate swinging in the wind and our fresh tracks leading out—

I ran as fast as a full-grown dragon can run. I had to stop him from seeing or calling out about our escape! But it was too late.

"Hey! What the—" said a hoarse voice. A voice I recognized. It wasn't my handler but it was the guy who had to haul our manure away every day. We had no choice but to leave the nasty mess in the corner farthest from where we spent most of our time. Barbaric!

Problem was, he was loud and drunk. I realized he could see where I was headed even if he couldn't catch me so I swung away to the east in the opposite direction from where my family waited.

There were few trees in that direction. Instead, it was mostly small farms owned by people who had little enthusiasm to have a big dragon training farm for a neighbor. No potential friends there, but I had to head that way.

As I lumbered along as fast as I could, the grating voice of the manure hauler faded. I dared to stop and look back. In the murkiness of the winter night, I didn't see any movement. He must have gone into the bunk house to rouse everyone.

This was my chance. I turned and headed west straight across the field for the forest. If I was beyond sight and earshot, they would think I continued east. But what if my handler knew better than the drunk manure guy? Why would any dragon head east unless he was stupid? The handler knew us better than that.

That meant there was even less time than I could hope for once he convinced the others to track us west. Maybe the manure workers' drunkenness would work against the handler's insistence to head west. Maybe slow things up enough....

But no such luck! Listening to any sound behind me, I thought I heard angry men's voices. Were they getting closer or farther away? I couldn't tell for sure until I neared the trees. The voices behind hadn't changed in volume. Had they split up with some heading east and the rest my way?

The volume increased slightly. I could even recognize some voices. Curses! With no option left, I headed southwest along the fence line. Would Springwind hear all this and take you children deeper into the forest around the other side to continue down the river valley? I could only pray to the Dragon God that she did.

I was not used to such exertion, my lungs burned, my legs weakened. If only I could fly! I tried desperately but my handler made sure our wings were always clipped close and our halters were tight so that flight was impossible.

I had always suspected they were going to eventually do something with us beyond pulling wagons, otherwise why didn't they just chop our wings off?

But none of that did me any good. The voice behind now became many voices to my left as some in front of me came into earshot. Surrounded!

Long-handled whips struck my back, neck, and face. I thrashed right and left and right again trying to fling off the whips and, better yet, strike men who ventured too close, but that didn't work. Drunk or not, they were experienced dragon handlers, so were the manure haulers, and soon I was hobbled by scores of whips wrapped around my body, tail, neck, even my snout.

Oh, for the gift of fire!

No wings, no fire, no such luck!

Exhausted I plopped on my belly and allowed them to strap a neck and body harness on me. With the combined power of many men and four large farm horses, they pulled me back to the barns.

One last swing of my head over my shoulder as if to fend off a whip, I listened for any action behind me that the men had found my family. I listened for the mother of my children's call.

Nothing. Only the harsh laughter and profanity of the victorious men who surrounded me.

At least my family had a chance to escape. Would they make it? Before they led me all the way back to the barn, they would discover the whole family was gone. Would that be enough time?

A Pause in Dark Cloud's Story

NINE

Sadness in the Cave

Skye stopped the telling of her father's story. Her voice was weak and I could hear a funny chuffing sound when she breathed. Was that the sound of a dragon crying? Was such a thing possible? I didn't know what to do. After a long minute, I couldn't stand hearing her cry anymore.

"Well, that's some story," I said trying to sound casual and forcing a yawn. "I'm sure you need a good night's sleep as much as I do. What do you say, we take a break and get some shut-eye? Maybe you can tell me more tomorrow."

She nodded and turned on her huge side and lay the way a horse does but so much bigger. The chuffing sound quieted and I felt a little better. Who knew dragons had such emotions?

I sure didn't. Lying on my side with my back to Skye, it took me almost an hour to quiet my mind enough to sleep like the dead.

The next morning wasn't much fun either. While first light started to chase away the darkness, Skye sat quietly near the cave entrance, eyes wide with a faraway look as if seeing something ominous in the fading stars.

While she sat, I was at a loss about what to say to her, so I went outside and looked toward Hilltop. I don't know what I thought I might see. At that distance there could be a large army falling into formation by the train station and I wouldn't be able see it. Still it was something to do.

After a few minutes, my eyes hurting from the strain, I saw unusual movement. Something flew over where I thought my town might be, circled twice, and then seemed to hover. I rubbed my eyes hoping to clear my vision, but I only made them water more. I stared at my feet for several seconds then lifted my face and tried not to focus so hard.

The hovering spot rocked back and forth slightly. The spot seemed to grow and the rocking motion increased. I realized it was headed directly toward us and could be here in minutes!

I rushed to the cave. "Skye! Come look, I think something is flying this way from town."

She straightened up, a look of surprise and then anger crossed her eyes and mouth. She stood and rushed past me faster than something her size should be able to move. I barely got out of her way.

"What do you think it is?" I asked.

She looked for a long time. *It's a gold dragon. I told you about them. The humans enlisted them as search and destroy forces in situations just like this where people on the ground cannot travel as fast as a gold dragon.*

"Why are those dragons *helping* humans? What is the matter with them?"

Nothing that good food, and comfortable quarters wouldn't solve, she sighed. *They are young and don't know anything different than serving humans. They aren't as smart as blue and silver dragons and they have a better life cooperating with humans rather than fighting against them.*

"But look at the way you and the silver dragons are treated! How can they—"

Like I said, they are young, foolish, and self-serving. They've never been allowed near enough to us to know any different than the lies the humans tell them to keep them in control. They are quick and can be deadly in packs, but they don't understand what being a free dragon means.

"What do we do now that one of them is heading right for us?" I asked.

Skye watched the gold spot continue to grow. *Actually, it's three of them. They must either know dragons used to live in this area or they can see the high cliffs and the potential caves for dragon homes. Let's return to the cave and get as far back as possible so they can't see in.*

"But won't they smell you, and me for that matter, without having to come in to know we're here?"

Maybe, but they are cautious as well as quick and deadly in battle. Skye thought a moment. *My guess is that they can't risk going back without a definite report we are here, otherwise the humans could trek all the way through the forest just to find us gone. They will not fly into a dark cave with too many unknown factors. They will set up surveillance while one goes back for a silver dragon.*

"Are silvers allowed to fly?"

Only with a gold rider. The silvers are not as set against humans as blues are but they are more rebellious than golds. A gold with a sharp herding hook can inflict fatal damage before a silver can shake a gold off his back.

"All for the price of a nice thick steak dinner, huh?" I said.

What?

"Food. Tasty, fancy human food. It's the best part you get from butchering cattle."

Yes, perhaps, Skye said.

"What if you drop me off a little ways from here," I said, "and I start making a big fuss to get their attention as they get nearer? I could act like I'm by myself and tell some story about how you tossed me away and left me? Can silver dragons talk and understand human language?"

Not very well. Among dragons the golds are like your dogs and farm animals. They can understand simple commands and use their own calls to convey very basic information, but that's all. The silvers are a little smarter and can actually communicate with blues but not much better than a child. However, there's a catch...."

"And what's that?"

The humans don't know if silvers can communicate any better than golds and they certainly have no idea blues are sentient, intelligent beings. You are quite unique because you heard me, not through your hearing, but in your mind. Dragons don't have the vocal equipment to talk like humans, but we think and blues communicate best from their minds.

She wasn't getting it.

I said, "My point was, can I talk to a silver dragon so that he understands the basic message that I'm alone here?"

Maybe. I never spent much time with any of them. What I know is mainly from my father and my mother, not experience.

"That's too bad. Well, we don't have any options because those guys are almost here. Come on, get me away from here."

No time, Skye said.

Dang, she sure was stubborn! "OK," I said. "Let's hide and see what the simple-minded golds do and then if a silver comes, I'll go to them and do the best I can."

I'm not sure if a big old dragon like Skye can shrug her shoulders, but it looked like it as she turned and walked back into the cave without another word. We made our way to the back of the cave beyond direct view from outside. I was able to find a nice little hidey hole, but Skye had to make do leaning against the wall with her head held high to stay out of the shaft of light from outside.

A few minutes passed like several hours.

I heard a sound resembling our farm turkeys flapping around to get over the corral fence at home. Shadows like flying lizards darted back and forth in the shaft of light through the cave entrance.

I looked at Skye. She looked back and nodded slightly.

Manure! Those things really flew fast and changed directions as easily as a hummingbird. Finally, one landed. Its shadow grew taller as it neared the cave entrance.

From my hole I saw its profile as it slowly stuck its head into the cave. It looked around and suddenly backed off, disappearing in an instant. I watch its shadow as it seemed to wave its wings about frantically.

The other two flying shadows descended. The three came together into one shadow blob with wings flitting about and high-pitched yowls sounding something like frantic coyotes. Then one shadow separated from the other two and grew.

A head slowly poked into the cave and turned to look directly at where Skye stood against the wall. The gold's scaly face broke into an evil smile, its teeth dripping drool. His face pulled back slowly and I saw his shadow approach the other two.

After sounds that were more like friendly banter among dogs, one of the shadows flew off. The other two separated and settled to either side of the cave entrance.

I crept to Skye and motioned for her to lower her head. It was a little startling to see that massive face only inches from mine, but I managed to focus on what I wanted to say. "Do you think we can go and take out those two guarding the cave?"

Skye smiled much like a teacher who had just witnessed a student finally solve a difficult problem.

I believe it would be worth a try. I can't move fast enough and you're not equipped with fangs and claws, but between the two of us....

Skye outlined her plan in terse directions. I nodded back, attempted a brave smile and started moving toward the cave entrance.

I stopped just out of the sight of the two golds. I took several deep breaths, not so much to gather strength and energy, but to gather courage—or maybe a stupid disregard for danger. I leaped into the bright sunlight and charged toward the dragons who were lounging on the smooth rocks near the cliff.

Their eyes widened almost to the point they popped out of their heads, but quickly changed to a devilish delight that one of their prey was running right into their waiting arms. That was my cue.

"Help! Help!" I cried out. "The big mean dragon took me captive! Save me before she comes and—"

I stumbled and fell on my face, not by plan, but it was unavoidable. Now I was going to become their easy prey after all. I scrambled to my feet and attempted to run toward them. At that moment Skye stuck her head out the cave entrance and tried to strike me with her head. I dodged, barely. I wondered if that was due to my quick reaction, or if she allowed me to dodge. In any case, the golds froze and backed off, probably afraid of the massive head and impossibly long neck of the blue that faced them.

I stopped and called out. "Save me! There are many blues hiding in other caves. I know where they are and will tell your handlers so you can capture them all. But if this big blue beast gets ahold of me, I'm done for and you won't know—"

Skye stepped outside the cave and made a show of trying to strike me again. I dodged in the opposite direction and fell on hands and knees while I reached toward the golds. Skye missed again, then as if to avoid capture, she retreated into the darkness.

I furiously crawled toward the golds but my hands could not stay ahead of my knees and I fell flat on my face. Eating dirt and feeling the sting of sharp gravel on my face and hands. I lay still, only my heavy breathing shaking my body. I saw the twin shadows of the golds creep near me.

What if they decided to kill me with a quick swipe of their sharp claws? What if they didn't understand a word I said? After all, they were dumb golds.

What if they don't dare come any closer to the cave in fear of the huge blue just within?

Rough claws dug into my upper arms and shoulders.

This is it. Here is where I die—

But they dragged me away from the cave. I remained limp in their claws. A few more feet and I would act like I was trying to get on my feet, but suddenly everything changed.

It got dark in an instant. The air filled with a mighty roar just before a rush of stale dragon breath washed over me. Two thin screams cut through my hearing inflicting a loud ringing in my ears.

A tornado tore up the ground all around me. I was flung against two hard boulders. The windstorm continued for a few moments and then it was quiet.

Deadly quiet.

TEN

Stuck in the Center of the Earth

The sun shone on me again. I opened my eyes and raised a hand to shade them from the sunlight. A large shadow loomed above me. For a moment it looked gold and black, but as my eyes and the dust cleared away, I saw blue.

Beautiful blue.

You can get up now. Slowly. You're rather beat up, little guy.

"Little guy, huh?" As I got up, I saw the mangled bodies of two gold dragons. I smiled, "Well, maybe so but we made a good team getting those golds."

Only for now, Skye said with a sigh. *The other will return on a silver dragon. That will be much more interesting because though silvers are about half my size, they are powerful, fierce fighters. I am still tired from pulling the train to Hilltop. I can't—"*

"Then we have to leave," I said. "Go back into the forest and disappear for a while."

Maybe you could, but my blue scales will stand out among the dark green and brown of the forest. And there's my scent. The gold will detect me the moment it flies overhead.

I sat down, dejected. "Then I don't know. What else can we do?"

Go higher. Across this narrow canyon, she said indicating the space between us and another set of cliffs, *is where my home cave is. I'm almost sure of it. It is deep and there's a long tunnel that leads deeper than I even dared go when my mother and I escaped to return here.*

"Oh, so you did get away?"

Yes, but it was difficult. That first night there was no time for rest. As soon as Springwind, my mother, heard the fight to capture Darkcloud, my father, she made us run as fast as we could. She and I took turns carrying my youngest sister and brother while the others ran with us.

Down the river valley to another large valley. Though my father had been taken to the farm years before with sheets covering his eyes, he could smell the changes in scents and the feel of the terrain as he went along. Be-

fore our escape, he told my mother about what he smelled.

He could tell when they brought him east along the river valley to the farm because of the way sun shone on his back. When he worked in the fields, it was easy to see the valley snake away from the forest along the west fence.

So, he knew which way to start. The trail of scents would have to lead the way back home from the bottom of the valley. Because of so many twists and turns, he had confused north and south. At the point of our escape, it was up to my mother to remember what he described and to reverse the order of scents and terrain.

The farther we went, the harder it was for the farm people to track us because the valleys and canyons that split off from the one that began at the farm were so numerous.

I was stunned the dragons could do something like that. I'm sure I could never remember that much detail even without a blindfold on. "So, you all made it back to near here. But then what?"

I'll tell you later. Right now, let's move across the canyon before the gold and the silver return.

Skye motioned for me to grab on to her harness.

"What?" I said. "Weren't you too tired to fly away when the golds were coming?"

We're only going to sail across the canyon now. The canyon splits in two just south of here. We'll bank left and land, then make our way to the cliffs you can see from here. There are dozens of caves. The entrance we want is not in sight from here. It will take the silver and the gold a while to find it because we'll go in from the back. They won't find our scent trail any time soon.

"OK, what choice do I have? I must go with you or end up in the stew for tonight's dinner," I said. I hoped she knew I wasn't trying to be funny.

We sailed down and, sure enough, there was the split at the bottom of the canyon. She glided along the steep incline for as long as she had momentum and landed on a ledge almost too narrow for her. Nearby was a small cave entrance behind a tangle of bushes.

I started to break away the biggest branches of the bushes to ease Skye's way into the cave's mouth, but she stopped me.

No, she said. *We want this cover to remain so those gold and silver dragons won't fly around here and find it so easily.*

"OK, it's your skin, not mine."

I slipped through and then had to cringe as I watched her force her way in without damaging too many bushes. I rearranged the branches to hide the evidence of our entrance and turned to her.

"Lead on. You're sure you know the way?"

It is etched in my memory almost as deeply as the memory of my mother's voice and my father's stories.

I grabbed ahold of her harness and stumbled along beside her and we descended into the most complete blackness and silence I had ever experienced. We would have no idea if the dragons or their human handlers came near until too late.

As we walked along, the lack of light and conversation between us made me more aware of the odor in the cave. It reeked of dust and a slight dampness, but there was something else. A metallic essence combined with something like burnt wood, but it wasn't quite wood. More like hot rocks and wood. That must be the scent of dragons, several years gone stale.

It seemed hours since we started our trek. I quit counting the skins and bumps my legs suffered. Finally, we stopped.

The absolute dark and silence oppressed from all sides like a giant hand squeezing an overripe peach. The slightest sound seemed so loud, the air pressure like hands beating my ears.

"What do we—"

Skye shushed me with a tight hiss.

"Sorry—"

Enough! her voice in my head said with deadly intensity.

I got the idea and stifled myself though I longed to share with her my fear and thrill at cheating death again.

The exhaustion of the last hour settled on me as if the ceiling had collapsed on me.

I awoke. Maybe hours later? I was lying on the dirt floor straining to hear if anyone or anything was coming our way. I reached in the dark to find the dragon. The sound of a restrained, deep sigh broke the stillness. It was Skye.

It's all right, she said. *I heard a noise far above some time ago, but nothing else. I expect they searched all the cave entrances, but finding nothing they may have given up. Let's give them a few more hours. If it's getting dark out, they will probably fly back to Hilltop leaving the humans no choice but to pursue us themselves. And that will take time. Two days if they hurry.*

"Good, maybe we can rest before—"

We can't assume it will take us any less time to escape here. As much as I want to stay in the cave of my freedom all those years ago... We must move on once it's dark outside.

"How can we possibly know when it's dark outside while we're stuck here in the center of the Earth?"

I have a good sense of time. Learned it pulling the trains. The train company insisted we always ran on time. Go back to sleep. I will also try to rest until I wake up when I sense it's dark out.

"Suit yourself." Who was I, the punk human kid to argue with a dragon the size of a barn?

I dropped off so fast, the next thing I knew was Skye nudging me. *Wake up. We must go back the way we came and see if it's clear for us to move out.*

"Did I ever tell you I'm not a morning person?" I laughed. "Can you beat that, a farmer's son not a morning person?" I laughed again and she didn't try to quiet me. I guess that meant she was pretty sure we were alone in this cave.

She was already standing so I had to bat my hands around in the dark trying to get hold of her. After tripping twice on big rocks, I located Skye and her harness. She started off and immediately threw me on my rear end. Since I was hanging on the wrong side of her, I ended up facing the opposite direction.

I heard an odd grunting sound from Skye. Dragon snickering.

"Glad you have your famous sense of humor back," I blurted.

If I don't laugh, I might... roar. And you don't want to hear that.

"Probably not."

With both of us facing the same direction, we plodded along for the second eternal period that day.

When eternity came to an end, the darkness around me softened, then the air flow changed. We were outside. Above, points of light marked the stars and even a sliver of a moon off to the southeast.

My eyes adjusted to the fact something could be seen again. In front of me I saw a dim, roundish glow.

Skye said in a low tone, *That's the cave we first hid in. Our gold and silver friends have settled in for the night. I must say they don't give up easily. But since they are over there, it means they haven't found this cave yet. We'll go back in a short ways and rest. You haven't had much sleep and I haven't slept at all since the night before.*

"Can you take a chance they won't sneak—"

Blue dragons have this ability to sleep with one half of their brains while the other is alert to certain things like the unwanted noises of a predator. Yes, we are prey, too, especially the likes of them across the canyon and to humans.

"Then why didn't you do that—"

Back in this cave? Because I needed my full attention to anything that warned they discovered us. Now we have some distance and they still don't know where we are. *If they really thought we were this close, they wouldn't be settling down for the night.*

"Well, that's welcome news. OK, you've convinced me. Don't wake me until morning."

I turned on my heels and went back into the cave.

Morning came and we watched from our lookout in the cave as the silver dragon and gold rider flew back toward Hilltop while two gold dragons, still awake, stayed behind. No doubt they would fly patrol looking for us while the silver dragon guided the humans back here through the forest. Soon the golds left to search.

I strolled down a gentle incline in front of the cave entrance. South of the canyon and its two large hills was the thickest part of the forest. I went back to our cave.

"I don't like the look of the forest south of here," I said to Skye. She didn't respond or look at me. "I don't think you could work your way through it without making a lot of noise and moving the trees around. Our 'friends' there couldn't miss the commotion. Couldn't we just fly away from here with the golds searching somewhere else for us?"

She sighed and shook her head. *No. All dragons are similar to predatory animals, as much as I hate to admit it. If we fly, we'll be a moving object in the sky. Any dragon could quickly spot us miles away because they can detect movement better than detail.*

"Oh, I never thought of that," I said. "My old dog can see a tiny bird moving around on the ground in the cornfield where I can't see a thing. But when I spot a neighbor's cat staring at us without moving from the top of the fence, my dog can't because he doesn't even know it's there unless I point it out."

Let's just stay here for a while longer and see what the dragons do. We're both tired even after a night's sleep.

Soon, the two other golds came back and seemed to settle down. They had been patrolling the area all the night before and that morning.

It was a little boring at that point but I mused on the fact that this experience had been tougher than my daily routine of farm chores, but somehow it was more fun. I wondered what adventures lie ahead, if we were to ever make it away from the caves and through the forest. Could we escape the trained dragons and their human handlers?

A second day and night passed. By the third night, Skye felt ready to finish the story of her father and how she came to be a machine pulling the Eastbound Dragon Train.

ELEVEN

The End of Dark Cloud's Story

Days went by as I remained captive at the farm with no word of my mate and children, which was good news, indeed. My fate was only important to the extent they remained free. Still, I wanted to be with them because of my love and longing and, especially, to help them return home and protect them from being tracked down and attacked by the farm guards.

At that time, I couldn't know whether we were of any value to the humans, alive or dead.

One night while a storm raged there was a commotion outside my barn. What could it be? Our family were the only dragons on the farm, but a sense of dread grew in the pit of my fire pouch. Soon the dread was justified as the doors burst open and my mate and the children were dragged in by horses.

My family all had thick coils of rough hemp rope wrapped around their necks and hobbling their rear legs. I wondered how long it took to pull them along with such restrictions on their legs. I was bound and tied to heavy posts at the corners of my tight stall, thus I was of no use to my family.

Each of my suffering darlings was tied the same way in their own stalls, the children two to a stall. Finally, the guards removed the neck restraints and my stomach turned as I saw wet trails of blood run slowly down their necks.

I roared and howled to no avail. If I could have uprooted those demonic posts, I would have killed all the humans and tore down the entire barn, but I was secured beyond my strength to break loose.

To calm the children, I sang old dragon songs of flight and joy. The heroic battle stories seemed foolish fantasy, but the desired effect was realized as the children drifted off to sleep. My mate looked at me as if to apologize for getting caught.

No, no, my dear, don't say it, I said. *If we had all been together, we would still be back here. As you can see, I am most useless. Please rest now. Let's go to sleep as if snuggled against each other.*

She murmured and lay down, placing her head as close to my stall as she could. I did the same and finally drifted off to horrific dreams of war, death, and destruction.

The next morning, I began to plan how we would escape for good.

A few weeks passed, and I feared we were all destined for the butcher's block, enough to feed all the farm hands for months when our flesh was properly aged. One day, the sun shining, the handlers untied us from the posts and allowed us to leave our fouled stalls. I did not envy the crew that had that mess of manure to haul off.

We were tied together instead of our legs hobbled. The long ends of the ropes were hitched to ten burly farm horses which led away from the barn and toward the first of several gates until we reached the front gate. Was this the day we were to be slaughtered?

Skye paused in her telling of her father's story. *At this point, there is no difference in his memory and telling than mine. So, I will tell the rest of this from my own point of view. Anyway...*

Outside the front gate there were no more fences nor other men besides those riding the horses that pulled us. No one followed behind carrying butcher axes or knives. I was mystified as was my father and mother. The children, in their innocence, delighted in the fresh air and warm sun—But I didn't. And neither did my parents.

Something was wrong.

Yet nothing happened when we reached the dirt road that ran beside the farm and headed east. This went on for hours as we passed other farms. Human children and adults turned their attention to us as we passed. The children ran to their fences and watched us both in mute fascination and fear. A few laughed and taunted us. Most of the adults sneered or turned back to their chores as we went on down the road.

I began to allow myself to relax and let hope germinate in my heart. I saw that my parents were not so easily lulled. But my head said this was not going to end as well as it might seem.

I was right, but it took several days of travel and nights sleeping under the stars. Though Spring had started, it was rather cold at night. Amazingly, our handlers allowed us to huddle together though we were closely bound to each other so that we couldn't do more than step away to relieve ourselves during the night.

The next few days brought us out of the hills and valleys onto a flat, bleak plain. We turned south for two more dreary days until we approached a place where it seemed as if hundreds of dozens of trees sprouted on the tabletop landscape. But these weren't trees. They were buildings.

A city! A city of such size, none of us could imagine how expansive it must be. There was no end of streets stretching off in all directions, crammed with stores, homes, and other buildings—some even stacked on each other three or four times. It was like a forest of people, buildings, streets, beasts of burden, and occasional little squares of trees and patches of greening grass.

We were led through wide streets bustling with all kinds of wagons, people, and huge buildings larger than the barns back on the farm. We seemed to avoid entering the heart of the city. Just when it looked like we were passing the edge of the city, we were taken into a barn twice as big as the one we left.

Inside, there were dozens of empty stalls large enough for blue dragons. We were carefully separated from each other with the children led off to stalls beyond our sight. My father, mother, and I were placed side by side, but we were tied to posts at each corner of our stalls.

Have courage little ones, Dark Cloud told the children. *You will surely be brought back to us. Keep your hearts hopeful and be glad for we are still alive.*

I sensed Father's thoughts because his emotion couldn't keep it from Mother and me. *By the Dragon God, it's a lie we're telling our youngsters, but what else could I say?* He looked at me in the stall to his left.

I couldn't hide my tears and how I wanted so badly to join my brothers and sisters.

Be brave, young lady, he said.

I had both fear and anger in my heart. With that confusion, I could say nothing.

All three of us felt the same thing. *What hope? What gladness?*

We were fed the usual dragon slop and left alone for the rest of the day. The next day, finally expecting a butcher to come with his big flat-bedded wagon to carry off our bodies, we were instead greeted by a dozen big-muscled men and one older bald-headed man who seemed in charge.

He looked at us as if judging how much meat could be harvested from the three blue dragons that stood before him. Then he directed the men to release me and lead me off to an arena within the barn several yards away from our stalls.

My father and mother watched as they took off the net of leather straps that restricted my wings. They stretched my wings and made short slits in them. I cried in pain though I didn't want Mother to hear that. Fortunately, I bled very little and soon quieted my cries.

In spite of that, Mother screamed profane words I had never heard from her, but of course the men had no idea she was saying nothing more than shrieking, unintelligible sounds.

I forced myself to remain stoic as they completed this task. Then they brought a huge halter and strapped it around me. Part of the halter passed over the first joint of my wings so that I could still flap them but couldn't reach full length to become airborne.

The older man struck me with a whip so long it could wrap itself around a dragon neck and stung mightily as it hit my skin and face. He pulled me to his ugly, sweating face.

"I swear by the Hound of Hades, you will do as I command or you'll taste more than the sting of my lash!" His voice was rough and his breath was sour and rotten.

He unwound the whip and raised it high.

"Rise you infidel beast! Fly! Fly!" he croaked.

Interesting that this human was much like our handlers on the farm. They thought we could not speak, but somehow, we would understand their speech. We had always played dumb with them at first, but enough cracks of those horrid whips and we did what they ordered us to do.

He repeated his command and I flapped my wings slightly. He repeated it again and struck my face and pulled the whip back as it coiled around my mouth. I felt wet, hot blood on my lips. I couldn't restrain myself any longer.

I roared in a manner unexpected from a young female, yet the old man struck again and commanded me, "Rise, rise up, foul reptile. Ugly lizard!"

That did it. I unfurled my wings and flapped hard. Droplets of blood flew everywhere. I swear some of the droplets spotted the men's faces around me and maybe even my parents like a light sprinkle of warm rain.

I reached the high rafters and brought my wings down stirring up a hurricane scattering dust and straw all around. But my wings could only reach about a third of their normal height. I felt myself leaving the ground but not very far above.

I struggled again and again. I was going to show that old big-mouth yelling above the hum of the wind I created, "Up, up, come on you spawn of blue demons."

I rose a little more but still short of my own height. The men held firm the leads of the ropes wrapped around my neck, halter, and base of my tail.

The man directed his commands to the men, "Now, you fools. Pull her toward me." They did. "Good! Now to my right." I drifted right. "Now left." And I eased to the left. I hated their control over me!

"Yes," he yelled and laughed. "That's it. It's going to work."

"Quit your infernal flapping, beast." He whipped my shoulders where the halter held my upper wings. "Pull her down, fools."

The men pulled me down but I flapped only harder. I thought I could escape these devilish men and crush the head of the hollering old man. But the men's grip was stronger and my wings were not free enough to fly out of this man-made cave.

Slowly they lowered me to the floor, and so I gave up and folded my wings on my back. Dizzy from the effort, I felt my ribs pulsing violently. I blacked out but I fought to remain standing. Finally, I flopped on my belly. Though I could barely see him in the fog of my brain, I glared at the old taskmaster.

The older man laughed. "I like her spirit! This one will do. And the halter works like a charm although I would like my tanner to make a few adjustments so she can fly with less strain yet not out of control."

The men re-attached the wing halters, cinched the restraining ropes and led me back to our stall. My vision barely clear, I looked at Father and Mother. I hated it, but tears overflowed my eyes. I slung my head to throw off the tears and slumped on the straw. It was all I could do to curl my head around and bury my face between the bed of hay and my belly.

My parents were silent. I heard my father mutter, *What in all the Hells of Humanity was that all about? Why allow her to fly upwards a few feet without being able to fly in the manner natural to a dragon?*

Why, indeed? I thought.

Humans are insane.

As the days went by, Father shared all of his story with me. I do not know why, but something told me our time together was coming to an end. I watched Father look longingly at Mother. His deep sighs told me he wanted nothing more than to have his beloved family curled up by him and Mother. Most of all, I wanted all of us to take to the air, return to our homes, and put all this horror and evil business behind us.

But I had no confidence that would ever happen. And it was no secret my parents felt the same.

So, I dreamed. Thankfully, my father told his and our story over and over again because it would be left to me to share it with our clan, our dragon cousins, and to those who came after us, whoever they might be.

Dark Cloud and Skye's Story Has Ended

TWELVE

The Problem with Hawks

I wish I could have said something to Skye that made her feel better about her father and mother, but I knew there was no point. It would be kind of a stupid thing to do.

I only sighed and stirred the ashes of our dying fire. After a while I lay down, closed my eyes and listened while she wandered around. She brought more dead branches, fed the fire for a few minutes and then lay down herself. Skye sighed more deeply than ever and grew so quiet I thought she had died.

I didn't bother to sit up and inspect her body. I knew she was alive because, I swear, I heard the sounds of her brain working, going over and over the story she had just told. And agonizing. Agonizing more than I have about my stubborn old Dad. In the name of the Creator, I actually missed my father right then.

Finally, I drifted off to a restless sleep.

It's rather strange to awaken in total darkness and wonder if it's morning or midnight. I felt around me and discovered I was alone.

I stood too fast, forgetting about the cave ceiling and whacked my head against a rock in the exact spot to scramble my brains.

"Ohh! That hurts like—"

Sorry, a low voice said. *I couldn't warn you quickly enough.*

"Skye. You *are* here."

I just got back from the entrance. Those gold dragons are still buzzing around. And though it's not yet sunrise, it will be soon. The humans might be here before midday. We have to leave.

"But how—"

Trust me, I can get us out of here, but it's going to take more hiking in pitch darkness. I can smell outside scents coming in from various openings in this cavern system. We'll just follow those scent trails until we find a way the gold ones don't know about. It'll be an easy exit for you, not so much for me, but I can stretch my body more than you think. It doesn't need to be a really big opening.

"I'm hungry."

Not now. We must move. You can eat after we're in the clear.

I felt like grumbling but I considered the fact this was more dangerous for Skye than for me. To those gold dragons I was just a dumb farm boy, not much use for anything. I kept the whining to myself.

"Lead the way, oh Big Blue One," I said with a smile she couldn't see.

"Hmm," she mumbled. I'm not sure she got the humor in my remark.

I added several bruises to my shins and cuts to my hands as I struggled to keep from slamming my face into the rocky cave floor. Every few yards, Skye stopped, sniffed deeply and moved on until we came to a junction of two tunnels. She sniffed again and led me to the left.

Finally, I noticed I could see the cave walls and floor a little. More of a dark gray than black. Still more light made it easier to avoid hazards as we came to a hole that seemed big enough for Sky to squeeze through.

I don't smell dragons, but to be sure I need to step outside and look.

"Here, I'll look out," I said. "Your big ol' blue head will be too easy to spot."

Though the dawn was barely glowing, I saw we were about fifty feet up a cliff above the forest with no way to work our way down without being seen by a passing gold. Back into the miserable dark cave.

She led us on another way. Another opening to the outside but she detected the faint odor of dragons. I looked. This time we were just below the original entrance, but we would still be noticed by the gold dragons. Again, back into the blackness!

Finally, after a lot of hiking, we found yet another hole to the outside. No scent of dragons. I peered at the forest below. We were out of sight of the dragon camp on the back side of the hill. The trees were only a few feet below us. An easy trail led to the forest floor.

I can glide while you walk down, Skye said with relief. *Little chance being seen unless our timing is totally wrong.*

I hiked along the trail while keeping my ears and eyes sharp for any flying gold lizards. I looked back and watched with fascination as Skye eased her head and neck out the cave entrance. She stretched and stretched her shoulders, chest and stomach until she could simply drop downwards and quickly glide between the trees. She beat me to a small meadow a few yards away from the hill.

Without a word we headed away to the southeast from the hills. As we went along, the forest became too thick for Skye to pass through. A meadow offered relief farther south.

As she crept into the open, I pulled on the tip of one of her wings. "No, don't go outside, they'll see you when they circle the hill."

No choice—

"Nope. Get back here in the shade and move along as close to the trees as you can. I know it's a pain in the rear and the ground is rough, but I'll walk along in the open and watch for a gold or silver flying lizard. I'll see them before they can see me at this distance. That way, you only have to cram yourself in among the trees for a little while to remain out of sight."

I don't know—

"Well, I do. So just follow my directions for once and let's get moving."

As we went along, I saw the gold shape of a flying lizard circling the hill. We moved deeper into the shade of the tall trees. Skye stretched and wormed and coiled her body around trees so that she would only be visible if someone stood where I did. I sat near her prone face and we rested a little while.

Her large eyes stared at distant clouds. Again, I marveled at the copper flecks in her golden eyes. After a while I stood to move to the clearing, but she nudged me with her snout.

"What—"

"Shush," she whispered in my face. *Give it more time. If anything drew their attention in this direction, they would circle for a long time watching for some sign of anyone's presence, enemy or not.*

Finally, I stood and sighed with impatience as I turned to face her. She nodded so I moved into the open space and examined the hills behind us. Nothing flying in the air meant we could continue along the meadow. Faster this time. After several minutes, Skye began to circle back to the west toward her old family cave.

The trees thinned so she could easily walk between them and the brush.

"Where are we going?" I asked.

Right now, back to my family caves—

"But that's right across from where we just left! What are you thinking?" I didn't mean to sound quite that rude, but, really!

It's the safest place for us and I can keep track of what they're doing. The golds aren't cunning enough to figure we would dare return within sight of the cave we just left. It's best for now, but the silver with them will not be so easily fooled. When we flew into this area, I saw that the forest continues to thin out to the south. You would be safe heading that way for a while, but not me.

"Maybe I should just go back to Hilltop so you can be free to deal with these gold and silver dragons," I said. I tried to hide the disappointment in my voice. "Besides, I've done enough to give my father a full head of gray hair and get myself in enough trouble to last until I'm thirty years old."

I don't think the dragons or the humans would allow you to go home. Unfortunately, they probably think you're dangerous because of me. You shouldn't have helped me to start with.

She paused for several seconds as she hurried along. Then, *I should have run you off that train platform. Why did I think a human boy could help me?*

"No, don't say—don't think that! I did this on my own. Gladly. My life was so useless and I was mad at my Dad. Madder than I should have been. But I'm learning a few things about life beyond little Hilltop. And besides, I think I've been helpful to you, and I don't want to miss out."

Skye stopped her headlong rush and looked at me.

Of course, you've been a help. I would be on my way to Portville in chains by now. But do you realize what this means if you continue with me?

"Yeah, I could famous!" I laughed, she didn't. "OK. I'll get in a lot of trouble helping an escaped train-pulling dragon. Maybe even get hurt or... die. Fortunately, I'm young enough to think I'll live forever and never get hurt... at least not real bad. So..." I laughed.

So, you should turn around and head west to Hilltop now, she insisted.

"No, I should stick with a, a friend. Probably the only real friend I've ever had. I love my Dad in a weird kind of way because he and my mother gave me life and a place to live and so on. My father doesn't listen to me. Down deep, I believe he means well, but he can be so mean sometimes. And unreasonable. I miss my mother, though I never had a chance to know her. This is my chance to do something on my own that matters."

Matters? Skye said with a snort. *It may matter enough that you'll be imprisoned or die!*

"Maybe. But it sure has been interesting—and kind of fun. So far."

So far, she said, giving me a look not unlike my father when I've spouted some stupid idea. *OK,* kid, *or should I say, young man."*

"OK? Kid?"

Yes. Onward and upward. We're getting closer. Keep your eyes and ears sharp for approaching dragons.

I shut my mouth as I realized we were deep into the danger zone again.

"What if they smell us?" I whispered.

I've been guiding us near fragrant bushes, trees, and weeds that can overpower our scent. There's also been a slight breeze blowing away from the hills taking our scent with it. Oh, wait. The wind is shifting. Let's back up and circle around farther west.

Finally, we climbed the far west side of the cliffs so that we were around the corner from the cave entrance. I peered across the gap between us and the distant hill and the cave where we had hidden earlier before dawn.

The gold dragons were still taking turns circling those cliffs like noisy crows and poking around trying to find other cave entrances. After several minutes, one of them flew back to their camp. Skye and I heard excited chattering, then they flew around to the southeast part of the hill, disappearing from our sight.

"I think they caught wind of our exit on the other side," I said to Skye.

This is our chance. Make your way around carefully while I fly into my cave. We can both move quicker if I don't have to carry you.

She took off, and I lost sight of her as she swooped down. I hurried along narrow ridges and crevices trying to stay hidden from anyone on the hill across from us.

I was surprised to find Skye curled up outside the cave beside a large rock.

"Why aren't you inside?" I said in a low voice.

There is a family of hawks who have taken residence in my family home.

"So?"

She looked at me like I was a dung beetle. *I hate hawks.*

THIRTEEN

Birds and Dragons of a Feather

I snuck into the cave and looked up. The light was very dim high on the walls, but after a few moments of adjustment, I caught sight of a crude nest of sticks and twigs balanced on a small rock shelf above the entrance. I heard peeping almost like baby chicks but the pitch was lower, the voices a little louder, more threatening.

Just over the edge of the nest, a large brown wing fluttered then slid out of sight. At least one of the parents was there. I stood in the shadows and waved my arms at the nest.

"Hey, birds. What's going on up there?" I said, trying to keep my voice from being heard outside. "Do you mind if we settle in? I know the owner of this cave, so don't get all possessive on me."

They didn't. In fact, there was no response at all from the chicks or adult hawk.

I went back outside and found Skye hiding in the shadow of the large rock keeping an eye on the hill across from us.

"I don't think the hawks care about us. I've been around hawks before. My uncle used to have a couple of trained falcons. We're too big to eat and too clumsy and stuck on the ground to concern them. Come on in. Just don't sit below the nest."

Skye uncoiled and slunk into the cave looking above suspiciously. *It's not that I'm afraid of them, I just don't want them to make a fuss,* she said unconvincingly.

I laughed. "Imagine how humans feel about being around you. Pretty scary if you're flying around loose. At least until people figured how to shackle you to trains."

Skye was not amused. I meant it as a joke, but I shouldn't have said that.

It's OK. Maybe with them flying in and out on trips to find food for their chicks, this will look for all the world like an otherwise empty cave. I just don't want them flying around my face and trying to attack us to protect their young. That's why I hate hawks.

"Good attitude," I said sounding like a couple of my sarcastic teachers when I was still going to school back in Hilltop. But since she mentioned the hawks seeing us as a possible threat to their babies, I kept a wary eye for the adults.

We settled back in and took turns watching the dragons across the way. It was actually a little less nerve-wracking outside compared to inside with the hawks. Soon the humans would arrive and things would really get interesting.

That night, as we watched our enemies flitting about their small campfire in front of their cave, we sat in the dark and cold of ours. A dry supper of raw nuts and some kind of wild potato didn't do much to bring cheer either.

I had poked around the cave before sunset and found old, castoff pelts of dusty gray fur I could use as a blankets. Skye told me they were probably the pelts the humans had used years before when they masqueraded as wolves to get the drop on her family.

The fur smelled rank and likely had fleas, but at least I was a little warmer.

To distract me from our misery, Skye continued her story.

Skye said:

Soon after the dragon handlers were sure my halters and straps were properly fitted to keep me under control and strong enough to pull a train, I was taken away to a smaller barn. Others my age were trained to the reins and whips used by the Dragon Train pilots.

Beyond the small corrals was an oval track laid with the same rails as actual railroads. Other blue dragons pulled short trains around and around as part of their training. As they got better at it, the trainers added cars to the practice trains.

Soon I was hitched to shafts on either side and connected to a cross bar secured to heavy eye bolts on the train. The harness clung tightly to my wings and ribs. The shafts restricted me more. I wanted to scream and thrash until I threw off those bonds.

Sensing my extreme discomfort, a crew of ten men surrounded me, each with a long rope attached to my harness in one hand and a long whip in the other.

A burly man watched from a small wooden box—much like humans' wooden outhouses—mounted on the front of the roof of the first train car. He held two thick reins from either side of my bridle in his left hand and a whip in his right hand. He cracked the whip and shook the reins.

Dark Cloud, my father had urged me to cooperate with the humans so that I wouldn't be punished. That was his fatherly concern for my safety and well-being. But I cared nothing about either, so I stood stiff-legged and held my head high, refusing to move.

The whip made contact on my spine between my shoulders. Though my back burned with pain, I didn't move.

Now two of the men pelted me with their whips. They stung like a horde of bumble-bees, but I stood my ground.

The pilot roared, "Come on, you worthless pile of dragon manure. Run or be beaten to the ground."

I proceeded to lay on my stomach and lowered my head to the railroad ties between the rails.

Now all ten men on both sides of me and the pilot unleashed a torrent, whipping me mercilessly for what seemed like an eternity but probably less than a half minute. The pain intensified until a dull ache set in.

They stopped at a signal from the pilot. He bellowed at me, "Get up now, you lousy blue beast or we'll beat you into unconsciousness."

I could barely raise my head. The beating had left me weak and nauseous. I struggled to unfold my left front leg, then my right as I pulled myself upright. I did the same with my back legs. Every movement painfully stretched my wounded skin as I fought to stay conscious.

I wanted to hold my head high, but exhaustion and pain wouldn't allow it.

The pilot gave the reins a powerful jerk. "Giddyap, stubborn worm!"

I pulled the train with what strength I had left. After an effort that nearly brought me to my knees again, the train began to roll. Soon I had to trot faster to keep from getting run down by the front car.

"Now fly, you fool, fly." the cruel man commanded.

I flapped my wings weakly. My back burned with pain but my wings felt fine. It was then I realized that none of the men had beaten my wings. I stretched them high and struggled to reach for the sky. If only I could break loose from the harness that restricted my wings!

My battered body lifted. For a moment my heart soared thinking I could climb, climb up and up until the train fell off, dropping those vile men and the pilot like rocks to the earth.

But, instead, I gained less than ten feet as I pulled the train faster. I aimed straight as the rails began to curve to my right, but the interlocked car wheels and the rails wouldn't let me pull the train off its tracks. My harness twisted and bound me tighter. The pilot's whip stung my left shoulder. Due to the heavy weight of the train, the shafts connected to my harness wouldn't allow me to stray too far to the right or left when I was pulling.

So, against my will, I had to veer right to ease the strain and pull the train around the right-hand curve more smoothly. The pilot laughed and uttered profanities as he insulted my efforts. The track straightened briefly but then the next right-hand curve approached. I tried again to pull left, but could not. After two more circuits of the small oval, I gave in and pulled right.

Now the pilot cheered and shouted, "She's learning to pull like a proper beast of burden. I swear my own horse cannot pull my carriage any better or smoother."

Somehow, I was not proud of my accomplishment. At that time, I only wanted to make the pain stop and to pull smoothly because I couldn't fight anymore.

Skye stopped her story and swallowed hard. I thought she had something from our meager, dry supper caught in her throat. Then I realized. I didn't spend much time around women except the occasional gatherings with family including my three aunts and a cousin five years older than me. Sometimes, when they spoke of something sad or, strangely enough, very tender and beautiful, tears would form in their eyes and they got all red-faced.

That's what I could hear in Skye's voice even though I couldn't see her face in the darkness. I understood. When I was going to school, bigger guys would tease or pound on me because I was younger and smaller. I would get so mad, the tears ran down my face to my humiliation. Then I would lash out hoping I could connect with one or two of their faces and, especially, their big fat noses.

Well, that's how I imagined Skye felt. She wanted to squash that pilot and all his mean assistants like they were cockroaches. But all she could do was pull the train as hot tears ran off her face.

To save her further embarrassment, I rushed to the cave entrance to see what those stupid, annoying dragons were doing across the gap. Dark shapes huddled around their fire. Some of the shapes were bigger than others, probably the silver dragons that had returned. My eyes watered from trying to detect human shapes. I didn't see any, but I couldn't be sure.

I turned back toward Skye. Keeping my voice under control, I whispered, "What do you want to do, just play cat and mouse with those stupid gold and silver dragons? And what of the humans? They may already be nearby ready to use their sneaky ways to figure where we are.

"Maybe you think they'll just give up and go away?" I continued. "But how do you figure that? Look how stubborn and smart they are to get a big ol' dragon like you under their control and pull a train."

I could barely see her silhouette, only slightly darker than the gloom of the cave. Her head was down for a moment, then she raised it and glared at me.

I did not give up so easily. Only did what was convenient at that time. I had been taken away from my family. I had no idea what was to become of them. Then they strapped a harness on me and beat me within an inch of my life so I could pull that cursed train and listen to the insults of that evil pilot.

I did what I had to do to make it through another day. That went on day after day. I realized I could use all my strength fighting them or I could use a little of my strength pulling the train. The humans are nasty, but they are very clever to devise a train that rolled easily and a harnessing system that worked well and felt comfortable if I only pulled properly. That battle was not one worth fighting.

In the gloom I sensed her determination. *There was another fight I had to save my strength for. And there was something else—or should I say* someone *else to consider.*

I saw her head waver a bit before she spoke.

There was Caerulus.

"That's a rather fancy-sounding name," I said.

Skye smiled. *Yes, it is and I told him so when we first met. This is a story I would rather tell now.*

"Sure, go ahead." I sat close to her, wondering who this guy was with the funny sounding name.

She told this new story....

FOURTEEN

Skye and Caerulus

After a week of learning to pull the train, I was taken to a long, low barn one night. The building consisted of a row of stalls made of tree trunks driven into the ground along both sides with large doors on one wall to lock in blue dragons. The back of the barn was solid to keep restless dragons confined to their stalls. The roof was pitched and large amounts of rough grass spread around the floor to keep the dragon poop from making a big stink.

Once I was left alone something heavy banged against the wall, over and over, between my stall and the next one punctuated by bellowing.

Hey, what's your problem in there? I said. *I'm not thrilled about being in here, either, but I'm not banging on your wall!"*

The commotion stopped. A low, male voice spoke. *Sorry, I didn't know anyone was on that side. I was... working out my frustrations.*

After a few moments of silence, I heard faint voices discussing something about a "new visitor" and "sounds like a female."

You can talk to me, you know, instead of talking about me! I said.

The humans have built this dragon barn with few conveniences, he answered. *But the one thing they don't realize is that we can communicate, so I was merely letting my other neighbor know I now had someone on this side as well.*

Oh. Well, I am not interested in anything but getting away from here, so unless you have a plan for escape, I am tired and wish to sleep.

Of course, he said. *Make yourself at home.* There was a pause, perhaps waiting for my response.

I had nothing to say.

He went on. *I'm sure you could do with a good rest.*

And that was it until the next morning.

A door slamming in the darkness startled me awake.

"Eat and be ready to work at sunup" a human voice yelled.

Not as loud, the same slam and command repeated next to my stall. And again, and again, on down the line.

I forced myself upright and lumbered to the wooden box next to the door. The same putrid smell of "odd meat" greeted my nostrils. The humans obviously thought hard-working blue dragons should be carnivorous—meat-eaters—and not omnivorous, able to eat anything. Though we were fed a lot of oat hay and a little ground meat in the barns with my family when I was growing up, here in the Dragon Train camps they fed us a small amount of oats mixed with horrid raw meat.

Perhaps humans preferred rotten piles of rats, dogs, and cows that died of old age, but dragons certainly did not. In fact, when we could breathe fire, we preferred our meat flash roasted. After all, we aren't savages!

But I was weak and I knew the day's work would probably be more intense now that I was in the Dragon Train Barn. I held my breath and swallowed the vile meal and hoped it would stay down.

I waited in the darkness for the trainer to come and lead me out. From a distance, I heard barn doors opening, the shuffling of dragon feet being led to the training grounds. Finally, next to me, my neighbor was taken, then my door opened.

It was still dark outside with only the slight blue of dawn marking the horizon. If I was a free dragon, I would have reveled in the beauty of such a morning. Unlike before, I was led to a long, fenced track by only one handler, a man I didn't recognize from my earlier training.

I whipped my head back and forth, searching the other dragon faces for some sign of defiance, a willingness to take advantage of this human miscalculation and stomp them into the ground. We could then take flight and escape even at low altitude!

But no one stirred. I hesitated. *Do I dare attempt escape alone? Why don't they—*

A voice, more like a whisper, interrupted my thought. *Don't. Look along the edge of the fence on either side of us. See those mounds topped by long tubes angled toward the sky above the track?*

Yes...

Those are human-made throats of iron that shoot fire. Unlike dragons they also shoot rocks and bits of metal. They will shred you into a thousand pieces if you try to escape. They call those cannons. The cannon shooters have a deadly aim. They won't miss you. If you don't die from the fall to the ground and the red-hot rocks and metal pieces, you will die a slow death as your blood and bashed brain soaks the earth.

Oh. That explains why no one is escaping. Thank you. Who is this sharing their thoughts with me? Where are you?

Right ahead of you. I'm your noisy neighbor. No more talk now. Later, in the stalls, we can get better acquainted. Today, we work, we behave, we eat that nasty slop so we can live another day.

I understand. Thanks for... letting me know about the cannon things.

We reached the track which did not actually wind around an oval but headed off into the distance across the fields and into the nearby forest.

That night, something big slammed again into the other side of the wall next to me.

Are you there? the now familiar voice asked in my head.

You have an interesting way of getting my attention, I said, more amused than the night before.

It's a way to release a bit of anger and frustration. I imagine the wall is my human handler and then 'bam!' Last night, I was just trying to get your attention because you looked very distracted when I peeked at you through the gaps in my front wall. As you can see, there are no gaps in the walls between us. They don't want us to have a chance to find a comrade even in captivity. However, they don't know we can communicate mentally.

Still, even then these low-class humans are very careful, I said. *Like I thought they were slipping up with only one of them leading us out this morning.*

Don't ever think you're going to get the slip on them.

My father did. When I was a youngster, he broke us free from a farm where we worked like horses.

Really? He must have been very clever and powerful.

He was. But the humans have learned a lot since then.

Where is your family? he asked.

I don't know. It's been a while and I—I don't like to think about what has happened to them. It's been so, so long since I've seen my parents, my brothers and sisters... I got mad at myself for getting emotional.

Sorry, he replied. *My story and nearly every other blue dragon's story here are about the same except for the escaping part. I guess the escape didn't last, but never mind. I just want you to know, we aren't separate and alone here—*

I don't really care about that, right now. I wasn't in a mood for baring my heart to some stranger especially a male stranger. Someone who said things and banged into walls to ease his frustration. I had my own troubles and I didn't need to take on his or anyone else's.

Understood. I just wanted to let you know that, well, I'm next door if you do want to talk or anything. By the way, my name is Caerulus.

Really? I never heard such a name before.

It means a shade of blue that's between the color of the sky and a dark blue. My mother was rather fascinated by human legends and poetry I'm afraid.

Hmm. My name is much simpler than that. I am called Skye. Not very original though the meaning is much the same as yours— I didn't mean to say that. I didn't want to encourage this dragon on the other side of the wall to think we had some kind of connection.

I went on before he could respond. *I am tired and want some quiet so I can sleep and clear my head and throat of that vile food they insist on feeding us.*

Understood, again. Good night, Skye. See you in the morning though you should be careful to not show any interest in me or any of the rest of us. The little wingless runt humans who have power over us must never suspect we can communicate.

As you say, 'good night.'

Night. A few terrible dreams, doors slamming in the darkness, putrid food, and come morning, more work pulling trains down the tracks. I could see this was going to be my life. Repeat. And repeat again.

After a week of this dreariness, my handler led me into Caerulus' stall. I balked and tried to back out. The sting of two whips assaulted me. One whip in the hands of my handler and the other from Caerulus' handler. I shook myself as hard as I could manage after a hard day of towing the train, but I was unable to shake off the tightened harness. I couldn't even strike at the men with my stunted wings.

Don't fight them, Caerulus voice yelled in my head. *Relax. They won't let you back out.*

This is not my stall. I don't want to be in here with you.

Maybe not, but they are obviously thinking of breeding more little captive blues to tow trains.

Not from me and not with you... or any other blue. I'm not some brood mare.

Maybe not in your heart or head. But they aren't asking for your permission. Just calm down and stay. I will not touch you or make you do anything you don't want to.

No! No! At once I felt helpless and about ready to burst with anger.

The cannons! Don't forget the cannons! Caerulus insisted. *Don't be a fool.*

I'm not a fool. I'm... I couldn't even think of what I was.

I slumped on the thick hay. I dropped my head in defeat. The whips stung again but abruptly stopped.

"Stupid blue cow!" my handler cursed. "Come on, let's get out of here," he said to the other human. "She's staying in here tonight whether she likes it or not."

Out they went slamming the massive door behind them. It was dark. And quiet.

That's that, my stall-mate said. *I'll just eat my half of the meal and you can eat once you've settled down. You can sleep right where you are. I'll be in the back corner—*

What's all the noise? a voice came from the other wall.

Nothing you need to know about, Caerulus said as he thumped the wall.

OK. No problem.

I heard Caerulus eat but when he was finished, I didn't stir. The last thing I felt like doing was eating. I was numb. No anger, no hope.

I finally went to sleep until the familiar slamming woke me up.

Another day and not even a moment of privacy before facing dawn-to-dusk training.

Skye sighed and smiled faintly as she paused in relating her story, then she noticed me staring at her.

What?

"Oh, I dunno, kind of nice to see you smile. At least, I think what I'm seeing on your face is a smile," I said. It was hard to tell with that big mouth of hers that reminded me of a serpent's.

Well, it won't last long. As the months went by Caerulus didn't seem to know the meaning of the word 'no' or a cold shoulder. In fact, he thought he was very amusing sometimes.

"How so?"

Skye's Tale Continues

Our handlers alternated between putting us together and keeping us separate in our own stalls. Maybe to create fondness in our hearts when we were separated. Didn't work with me. For a while....

One night my head was buried in my trough when Caerulus banged against his side of the wall between us. Like an idiot, I looked over at the wall. There was a tiny crack between the thick posts his slamming had opened. He passed a clump of wildflowers through the crack.

What do you think I am, some lovesick cow who'll accept a cheap gift of wildflowers for dessert, I said, not too kindly.

Ah my love, if only I could uproot the beautiful flowers from the head trainer's garden! But this is the best a captive dragon can do. Please accept—

Pooh! Keep it and chew it yourself. Maybe it'll cure your wrongheaded thinking that I'm actually interested.

Ah, now that is good to hear, he said as he chuckled. *At least now you're acknowledging that my attempts are to get you interested... in me.*

If I could have passed gas at that moment, I would have let go, but the meager rations they gave us during the day could produce no such thing. I flapped my wings in an effort to dismiss him, but he wasn't discouraged.

No matter, Sweet Skye, I will endeavor to steal a red blossom from the trainer's garden someday and then you'll realize how serious I am.

No, just how funny you are, I said, immediately regretting even that slight compliment.

And so, it went until one day, late in spring, I accepted an offer of a pile of acorns he had accumulated from around the trunks of oak trees along the edge of the training grounds. Acorns! I love nuts, such a rare treat especially in the camp.

He knew he had me. It was hopeless for me to continue my game of avoidance and half-hearted rejection. The only part of it I despised was the fact the trainers were pleased to see us growing close. Of course, they wanted us to breed fresh, captive-born blue dragons that didn't require breaking their will like they had to do with us.

I hated that! So did Caerulus, as it turned out, but as he said, *I don't care what they want us to do, I cannot deny my attraction and deep feelings for you. Even among free-living dragons, I would pursue you with all my being.*

Oh really, cut the romantic poop, I said trying to convince him I was only relenting because of exhaustion. *Still...*

Yes, still... he echoed.

So, it went. The one nice thing about our developing relationship was that we could occupy the same stall and share warmth on cold nights and no longer sleep alone. Because I missed my parents, brothers, and sisters, that helped.

Soon children came as five more years passed. But before the children came, we were ready to tow trains and our few days together were split up by bouts of running our routes for several days at time. We only spent about ten days a month together as we rested between routes.

My route from Forest Town to Crossroads, passed through Hilltop. I ran that route four times a month, sometimes more often when other dragons were worn out and slaughtered once their usefulness passed. But the humans never allowed Caerulus to run that route, I guess on account of some fear we might plan a means of escape, though I don't know how we could have done that.

In any case, one of us was always at the Blue Dragon Barn in Portville when the other ran their regular route. That way the children would have one parent with them until they were old enough to be taken away for training. The time for training our eldest was coming once he reached six-years-old.

Among other captive blue dragons we heard and passed on whispered stories about lands to the far north where dragons fly free and humans respected them. Could it be possible?

My mate and I vowed to find a way to escape with our children before they were taken from us. But what to do? Could either of us be as clever as my father, Dark Cloud?

The chance came when I became ill on the way to Hilltop a few days ago. I've heard humans get a thing called a "cold." I think I got the dragon's version of a cold. I found it hard to breathe during the climb to your town. My throat hurt as if burned though I have not spewed flame in ages.

I was exhausted by the time we reached Thistledown. But the Dragon Train conductor would not allow me to rest or have someone bring in a dragon to replace me to take the train on to Portville.

I pulled the train with everything I had. If I collapsed completely, I would be killed and thrown off a cliff or burned on the spot. I couldn't leave Caerulus alone with the children to raise and no hope of escape. As you know, I made it to Hilltop but could go no further without dying.

Only when you came along did my feverish brain conceive a plan. That, and your helpfulness, gave me such new hope I recovered from my exhaustion along the way during our escape. The long nights sleeping in these caves have refreshed me.

And now, my story's done and the challenge waits before me. How to get back to the Big Barn and release my family?

At that point, Skye looked at me as if she were expecting a mere mouse to stand on its hind legs and fight a wolf pack. I wanted to protest but, how could I?

What would I do if it were me and my loved ones in captivity? Even though all I had was a grumpy father and some aunts, uncles, and a few cousins who I wasn't all that close to... should I give up and run away? Tempting, but I could tell Skye was not that kind of person, or should I say, dragon.

"Sure, let's see what we can do," I said as my voice squeaked the same way it did a couple years before when I was still a smooth-faced boy. I know I looked more or less like a man and wasn't much smaller than my father, though his muscles were way more powerful than mine. But...

But, of course, I had to offer my help. What could happen? Well, I could die, maybe in a spectacular way, though more likely, pathetically.

An expression crossed Skye's face. I think the big blue dragon wanted to cry, but I couldn't tell if it was appreciation or fear of disaster. But she somehow reached deep inside and smiled as she said, *Thank you. It will be a big risk. I fear it is too late to find my family together because the humans will certainly punish Caerulus for my—our actions and separate the children from him.* Her voice trailed off into silence.

Not knowing where my breath or voice came from in spite of my rising panic, I said, "I pledge to you we will find a way to rescue your mate and children."

I sighed.

Skye sighed.

Now what?

FIFTEEN

Bait and Switch

After we lay down for the night, it took me quite a while to finally drift off into a restless sleep full of horrifying battle scenes where Skye, other blue dragons and I were burned like rats in a brush fire. After a particular frightening dream, I awoke as Skye slipped out of the cave. Although I was groggy and could barely keep my eyes open, I forced myself up and followed quietly.

From the mouth of her family cave, I watched as she stared at the star-filled sky. I thought I heard her sniffling. A subdued sound, almost more imagined than heard.

I had an idea she was thinking of the times when dragons could fly freely and scorch anyone who tried to harm them and take their freedom away. Abruptly, she turned around. I thought my spying was discovered but I stayed hidden in the shadows. She must not have seen me because she rushed past me and searched the back of the cave as if trying to find a treasured item.

Moving behind a rock twice my height, she stepped into total darkness and disappeared.

I rushed to the shadow behind the huge rock. It was an entrance to a low tunnel. I marveled at how she must have folded double to pass into the emptiness.

Sounds echoed from deep inside, but I feared to wander in behind her. I returned to my musty furs and wrapped myself in an effort to get warm again and to forget what I saw. I had the intuition that this searching in tight tunnels was none of my business.

After what seemed hours, she reappeared.

She approached me, not as if she expected me to be asleep but that she knew I was wide awake.

We may have waited too long. My Caerulus and babies probably don't have a chance—

"No, we must go now. There is still a chance. The humans have only been searching for us a couple of days. They know there's no way we could be on the way to the Big Barn, wherever it is. Even now we're not too far from Hilltop so I figure your barn is a long ways from here."

But—

"No, really," I said. "Those gold and silver dragons are pretty sure we're still here in the area, otherwise they would have left yesterday. Wouldn't it take a while for humans to return to the Big Barn. Aren't they just hoping—"

You're the one hoping! she blurted out. *We can't be sure.*

"No, we can't but we have to take the chance. Right now, let's sneak out of here and hit the skies. You can take me with you. I don't care how cold it is or how much I poop in my pants hanging on to you flying in the deep of night, we have to go now!"

Or...

"Or forget it," I said without sympathy.

We can't fly in the night. I'm not familiar with the wilderness territory beyond here. We have to fly directly to the Big Barn—but I don't know exactly where the barn lies. It's too risky and will take too much time to fly along the train tracks.

"Darn! You're right. Yet we have to fly, no time for anything else. Then we'll figure where to go. But maybe... Maybe I have an idea so we can fly right after first light." For once, I felt a kernel of hope build in my heart. That or it was the delusion of a punk kid, as my father would say, who thinks he knows everything!

I looked around the cave, trying to think of something, *anything*. Then I caught sight of the old furry skin I slept in.

"I've got an idea!" I cried too loudly.

Shhh. Don't make it too easy for the golds who are listening for something out of the ordinary.

I stifled myself and pointed to my make-shift blanket.

What? Skye asked.

"My blanket. It smells like an old dead dog or something. And that's it. It can hold a lot of scent. I need you to pee on it so it takes on as much of your scent as possible. This is going to be our ticket away from here."

In truth, I had no idea exactly what I was going to do, but we had to draw them away from here so we could take flight without being seen.

If a dragon could make a disgusted face, she did it right then. Or maybe I just imagined it. Anyway, she took the fur away from me and carried it off to the back of the cave. She stopped, turned back, and glared at me.

Turn around. I'm not going to relieve myself with you watching. I had enough humiliation when I was under the trainers' watch all the time.

"OK," I said and turned around to gaze out the cave trying to think what I was going to do with a wet fur blanket. I wouldn't be using it for a blanket anymore. Maybe there was another one around here I could take with us when we left.

Trying to ignore the sound of her peeing, I continued looking outside as one of the hawks screeched above us.

"That's it! We can get the hawks to take the blanket and drop it off somewhere away from here. That will draw them away... I think."

Skye came to me, barely holding the blanket by a corner. I took it by another corner from her. Yep, it definitely had a fresh odor of urine about it. Reminded me of cow pee.

I tried unsuccessfully to keep the wet part from touching me, but would I rather be captured by the gold dragons and humans?

I found some notches in the cave wall below the hawk's nest. They would have to do for hand and footholds. I climbed on shaky legs as my fear of falling increased. Finally, I was only a few feet from the nest when one of the adults noticed me.

Moving to perch on the edge of their nest, the hawk screeched at me. It shifted around on the rickety edge of woven sticks and cast-off feathers. Behind it, I saw the other smaller adult hawk. The bigger bird nearest me, which experience told me was the female, looked like it was ready to attack.

"Wait," I called out, wondering if the bird could understand anything I might say to it. The female stopped a moment, probably curious about what the stupid human wanted.

"We need your help," I continued. "If you can understand me like Skye, the dragon down there, we want you to take this away and drop it somewhere to draw the dragons away from here."

The hawks twisted their heads and cocked them at different angles as if thinking about what I said.

Below, Skye's thoughts directed toward the birds came through loud and clear. *Take the blanket away toward where the sun sets. It will mean we will leave you and your family alone in this cave. My little friend here will bring you food for your fledglings.*

"Why me? Dang it! First you make me carry this wet stinking thing up here— Oh. I get it, you can't go anywhere without our golden friends seeing you. OK. I'll do it, but what do I hunt for?"

Anything that creeps upon the earth.

"Yeah, I knew that. Sorry for whining so much." I turned back to the female hawk and offered the blanket. It took the blanket even more delicately than Skye had. Both hawks flew off the nest and left the cave.

"Hmmm." I said. "I guess you got through to them. Good job."

Thanks. And now you need to go hunting.

I climbed back down and picked a few smooth rocks that fit well in my hand. In spite of what my father used to say, I guess I didn't waste my time slinging rocks at squirrels and anything else that moved around the farm. I was about to prove him wrong.

Grabbing another scrap of wolf skin as camouflage, I crept out of the cave and down the cliff under the cover of darkness. Below, in the dimness of starlight, I found what I hoped were a few animal holes. I settled in to watch for something to leave or enter the holes so I could kill it for the hawks. At least this would pass the time until we were ready to leave.

I wondered how Skye expected the gold dragons to find the blanket.

The sun began to color the sky to the east with a deep blue, then a grey the color of dead animal eyes. I spotted a few ground squirrels and lizards coming to warm themselves in the sunlight.

I placed a round rock in my sling and spun it. A few well-aimed throws and I had a pretty good pile of dead animals suitable to feed hungry fledglings. Forming a bag with the wolf skin, I loaded my kills and climbed back to the cave.

About that time, the hawks returned making all kinds of screeching, clucking sounds when they saw the pile of dead squirrels and lizards. The two predators made several trips flying the prey to their demanding fledglings.

"What about that?" I said. "I think they're pleased with my hunting prowess. Me, a punk kid compared to hawks!"

Don't get too proud of yourself. I sneaked a peek at the pair as they left the cave. They stayed out of sight of the golds as they circled around to the west side of this hill and then came from the northwest, passing your blanket back and forth between them. When the small dragons caught sight of them, the hawks dropped the blanket onto a thick tangle of small trees and bushes. As the hawks flew beyond sight, the golds went over and I could tell they got close enough to catch a whiff of the blanket.

"Great! That should keep them busy for a while," I said.

They were tearing around that thicket trying to get at the blanket or what they probably thought was a piece of my hide. But they won't waste their time for long with their short attention spans. Let's fly.

I grabbed her harness near the saddle bag, made sure it was tight around her body while keeping her wings free, and wedged my feet and legs in between the straps and Skye's body.

"OK," I cried and we took to the sky.

I wasn't scared like before, but as we rose the air grew colder and our speed increased. I hung on tighter than ever. Skye wouldn't be able to keep up this pace since her wings had been clipped by her handlers. But she labored mightily to leave the golds behind. At least, I hoped so.

Soon, Skye dropped elevation where the forest thinned and the hills flattened and spread across wide plains. The land tilted downward as we continued east toward the area called the Nulland Plains.

Though I'm not sure of the exact location of the Big Barn, the more I thought about it this morning, the more I realized it must be beyond the edge of Portville close to the countryside somewhere north. It didn't seem very far when they moved us from the holding corrals in Portville to the training oval, and then to the camp where we were outfitted to tow the trains. They always took us in big wagons with no windows, but it wasn't more than a few miles at a time. Now, as I think about it, I think they took us farther and farther north.

I only traveled along the Dragon Train tracks in and out of Portville on my route, but I sensed the directions as any dragon can. I also noticed how the forests thinned and the trees changed from pine and juniper to oak, elm, and sycamore. Then we crossed Nulland before I neared the city. I will follow the trees below us along the long slope. Surely, we will catch sight of the city and surrounding villages. Maybe I can retrace our travels as they moved us along to the Dragon Train camp.

"I sure hope so." I wondered when and how all of this was going to end. And then what? Back to the farm and a father mad as hell? Maybe not!

Skye interrupted my wandering thoughts. *This morning I did not see a silver dragon with the golds, but now, for sure, a gold will go back to the humans near Hilltop and report. The silvers will surely come and sniff out the trick we have played on them.*

The silver dragons are no match for blue dragon intelligence, but they will quickly realize I came back to my cave under the golds' noses. I must do the next unthinkable thing and return to the Dragon Train camp. We must hurry.

"Actually, *you* must," I said, being a bit of a smart aleck. "I'm just along for the ride. In fact, you can drop me off to lighten your load if you want."

No, my intuition says if you and I have worked well together so far—

"But I've done next to nothing!" I said.

I don't understand it, but somehow your presence with me in the last few days has transformed me. My father and mother were great fighters, but that was before I was born. Of course, his stories—I can't explain, but I'm not leaving you behind. Especially in a wilderness with no telling what kinds of beasts wandering about. Bears, lions, wolves....

It was settled. I would have appreciated a break from clinging to the side of a flying blue dragon, but I, too, knew time was running out on us.

We flew on.

SIXTEEN

Unscheduled Stopover

The Plains of Nulland were now more desert than plains, though a handful of farms below made my father's patch of small mountain land look like a green paradise. What did these poor people grow on such barren land?

Ahead in the afternoon light, I saw scattered stone huts of a run-down village. Low hills to the north on the edge of the village offered a clump of trees and a rocky outcrop where we could land unseen.

Stiff fingers, arms, and legs made it hard for me to let go of the harness and step on solid ground. Used to the gentling rocking of Skye's flight made the ground seem strange to my senses. Skye was so exhausted, she lay flat on her stomach, her tail stretched out, her chin also on the ground.

Finding a patch of grass at the foot of a tall, smooth rock, I sat, leaned back and went to sleep.

I awoke as the dull light of mid-afternoon colored the sky and land. At the same time, Skye opened her huge eyes, looked at me as if she didn't recognize me for a moment, then cracked a never-before-seen dragon smile.

Feel better after a short nap? she asked.

"Better but not great."

Good enough.

She stretched and rose with such ease I swear she might have slept for a full day. But I knew better.

She crept to the top of the rocky outcrop and gazed at something in the distance.

I can barely see the city, Portville. We shouldn't approach it, but we must if I'm to find the camp. I could fly north and wander around, but that would only confuse me. I have never flown above the camp and wouldn't know what I was seeing until we were spotted.

In fact, I can't take the chance right now to fly anywhere near or around the city because it's a no-fly zone for all dragons, even golds and silvers. Most people don't like seeing dragons in the sky, you know.

"Hmmm," I mumbled. "Never thought about such a thing. I trust you're right though." I crawled next to her to observe a city I had only heard about from a few Hilltop villagers who had visited the grand-sized village.

It was hard to imagine I was seeing so many homes, buildings, wide streets, hundreds of smoke trails rising from the man-made conglomeration. It just looked like a pile of posts and boxes from that distance. All that and more that I couldn't identify because I was a mere ignorant punk from a village that didn't even rate a stop by the Dragon Train.

I said, "Wow! I can't take all this in. So, what are we going to do now?"

I just had to get here. Now here we are. But no solution for how we remain unseen on the ground or from the sky. Even at night or if we could travel in exactly the right direction. If I could only enter towing a Dragon Train...

I swear I saw a light flash across those eyes and it wasn't from the sun shining on her face.

Unless—

I waited. "Well, unless what?"

She backed down the outcrop and coiled her massive body around to face west. *We fly again. Grab on and save your strength for later.*

"What—?"

There was no answer. I had to scramble to latch onto the harness before she would have left me alone on the hill.

She flew southwest without a word until a long straight line stretched due west into the distance across Nulland. The line disappeared into the dark green of an oak forest.

"Train tracks?" I asked.

Yes. We're going to take a train. I feel energized. I believe I can tow a train into Portville.

"Oh no. You haven't gotten near enough rest and your brain is getting whacky. How can we—"

Leave that to me. But I'll need your help.

She swooped just above the few trees dotting the landscape. Her head was elongated and focused straight up the tracks. I looked and saw it.

A Dragon Train approaching.

Skye dipped her left wing far enough that we whipped around and headed at an angle away from the tracks and back toward Portville. Ahead, a sharp curve in the tracks wrapped around a clump of trees. We landed behind the trees.

I will explain all in a few minutes, but right now, help me cover the tracks with some broken branches.

As she said that, Skye ripped up small gangly trees that grew near the tracks. In a flash I got what she had in mind. Could possibly she plant that idea in my head without conveying any words with it?

Or maybe I was starting to think like a smart dragon. If she was reading my thoughts, she didn't disagree with that realization, so I took it as a "yes."

I stacked the branches all over the tracks making the rather sad bunch of trees look more ominous than they actually were. The train could probably blast right through the pile. Skye dragged a few bigger dead tree trunks to the edge of the tracks. With the way I piled the fresh branches on top, it looked like a couple of huge trees fell across the rails.

The familiar clickety-clack of an approaching Dragon Train broke the silence.

Hide! Hurry, hurry! Skye demanded. *Hide right here on the ground behind the small trees so they can't see you.*

She then slithered back around the clump of trees.

I sensed her thoughts from a hidden place in her mind, as she directed me to fulfill her on-the-spot plan.

"Brilliant," I said and scrunched down more to make myself invisible.

The roar of the train on the tracks grew to match the sound of a mighty storm. I peeked from behind my hiding place and saw the train burst around the curve.

As the train dragon saw the blockage on the tracks, his eyes grew large, his mouth opened wide making a sound like a monster snake hissing. He flapped his wings in reverse and raised his chest, feet skidding on the tracks. His wings pushed and pushed forward as if trying to lift the pilot's cabin and jerk it up and behind the train's forward momentum.

The pilot screamed, "What the blazes? What the blazes?" cursing the seemingly stupid reaction of the dragon. His face turned from bright red to white as he saw what the dragon saw.

He quit whipping the dragon and pulled on the reins so hard, I swear it would have strangled the dragon if the great beast had not raised up and over the pilot's cabin.

The train came to an agonizing stop only a few feet short of the fallen trees.

In moments, the pilot piled out of his cabin while the conductor was already on the ground, pulling on his red coat, and running forward. Behind him a few curious and rather angry passengers flowed from the cars to see what outrage had brought the train to such a brutal stop.

The pilot yelled back at the conductor. "Get Clod, my crew and a few able-bodied young passengers to help get the trees off the tracks. Tell the rest to shut the Hades up and get back on the train."

The conductor turned around and motioned to a few well-muscled young men behind him. "You guys get over here and help the pilot. The rest of you, back on the train. Nothing to see here. We don't want anyone to get hurt. Come on, hurry and please be quiet! We have work to do!"

When many of the older men and women simply stood around watching, the conductor stepped up his appeal. "Back. On. The. Train. NOW... Please."

They slowly followed his command.

Suddenly, a big mean looking guy appeared. It was Clod from the search party back in the Emerald Forest near Hilltop.

Oh, Lord of the Dragons, no! I ducked out of sight. I watched Clod like a hawk zeroing in on a rodent. He wandered around surveying the area intently.

While the men gathered around the trees and branches to move them, I slipped out and worked my way along the edge of the group which paid no attention to me. I looked back one last time and saw the pilot whipping the train dragon to make him help move the trees. He lifted one of the heavy trunks with his long neck as the men tipped it off the tracks.

When I reached the conductor, I ran past him saying, "OK. OK. I'm going. Sorry, you can't blame a boy wanting to see what's going on."

"Yeah, well hurry up, bum," he shouted.

I went into the first car just behind the pilot's cabin. Some were looking out the windows while a few of the older men, dressed in fancy suits, were telling the others about the fallen trees. Beautifully outfitted women were enthralled by the men's accounts. I must have stumbled into some kind of high-priced car with a bunch of mostly older, rich people in it.

The conductor was right because I felt like a bum with my matted hair, dirty hands, and no doubt stinking body. I scurried to the back of the car before people could get a good look and whiff of me. I stationed myself near a window to see what was going on outside.

In less time than I expected, the men who helped clear the tracks headed back to the other cars. With a lurch, the train started to move. I had never ridden in anything more than our farm wagon, so the quick buildup of speed this close to the ground was more than I expected.

Through the door at the front of the car, Clod walked in surveying the crowd of passengers.

I tilted my face and turned away as he brushed past, knocking me against one of the seats. He looked into my eyes, I fought off fear and stifled my urge to whimper.

I sensed a moment of recognition in his face, but then his eyes went blank and he moved on. How long before he would make the connection that I was the punk in the forest with Skye?

I looked about desperately for some place to slink out of sight and saw a few young people about my age. I started to sit in an empty seat among them, but one of the bigger boys sneered at me. He was dressed in a shiny black suit with a black hat cocked at an angle that fit the way he looked down on me like I was vermin.

"Get out of this car, rat's face." He pointed his finger at me. "You obviously don't belong here. Get out now or I'll report you to the conductor and you'll find yourself walking to Portville!"

I could have taken him with his smooth clean hands and boyish face, but at that point reluctance was the better part of valor. So, I ducked my head and mumbled, "Sorry, sir. No harm meant. I got confused."

I turned and fled for the back of the car as if going through the door.

As I reached the back, I saw an open door on my right to an indoor toilet. I rushed in and slammed the door behind.

Nobody in there! I locked the latch and sat to wait.

A few modest knocks on the door occurred during the next few minutes. "Sorry, not finished yet!" I called out.

After a moment, footsteps faded away.

The train begin to move again. Now was time for *me* to move.

SEVENTEEN

Tricky Footing

Out the back door of the train car, steps lead off both sides of a small landing. A small wooden ladder attached to the narrow back of the train car reached the roof. That was my way forward without being observed.

At the top of the ladder, I searched all around. No one visible either forward or behind me, no one on the ground, either. The wind from the speed of the train burned my eyes. The car had a rounded roof. Dang it. If I didn't have to crawl across that roof, I would have gladly skipped it.

After flying in mid-air while hanging onto Skye's harness, I thought this wouldn't be scary at all. But this close to the ground, as the trees and landscape rushed past, paralyzed me. Maybe if I looked toward the horizon and not at the ground.

It worked. With the few distant hills and scattered trees seeming to pass by slowly, I mounted the mid-point of the roof. I crawled, careful to lean slightly right or left as the car bobbed and weaved. If I leaned too much, I would roll right off. At the front of the car was another ladder to the landing. I didn't have the nerve to jump across to the pilot's car, so I climbed down.

Right at that moment, of all people in that rich people's train car, that sneering boy came out and looked me in the eye.

"I thought I saw some vermin crawling along the top of the roof!" he yelled over the clickety-clack of the train wheels.

"How could you see me?"

"Your shadow, idiot," he laughed and pointed to the left side of the car.

There, on the light-yellow landscape whizzing by, was a shadow of the train cars allowing a clear view of anyone crawling on the roof.

"I saw you slip through the back door and watched your shadow," he said. "You're pretty good on your hands and knees—for a punk!"

I could have wiped the smirk right off his face, but that would only bring more attention to me.

"Look," I said. "I got on the train very early today. I was supposed to get off at the last stop, but I fell asleep.

And then the trees across the tracks caught me by surprise. Once we got rolling again, I thought I might get off here and walk back home by taking a shortcut across the Nulland Plains."

"You can't jump off with the train going this fast. You're full of beans, low-life!"

"You're not making this easy, blast it. Let's see how you do if *you* fall off the train right now."

With that, I hooked my right foot behind his feet and pushed him off the landing. He grasped for something to hang onto, but dropped too fast to grab anything. I peeked around the edge of the car to watch him roll on the ground numerous times before he finally came to rest.

He didn't move for several seconds, and a wad of fear formed in the pit of my stomach. He was a jerk but I didn't want to kill him or even injure him, at least not too much.

To my relief, he moved slightly. Then he tried to scramble to his feet but stumbled to his hands and knees. Finally, he stood up. Weaving crazily, he ran along the tracks, yelling. He disappeared from view as the train rounded a curve.

If somebody saw him, they would tell the conductor. I didn't have much time.

I climbed the ladder and studied the back of the pilot's box that rose about three feet above the roof of the car.

Skye had told me what to do if I had gotten this far. I sure hoped I could remember everything. One thing she hadn't explained, but I figured for myself, was that the little four-foot square box was placed high enough to allow the pilot to see over the dragon and know what was ahead.

Just like the train Skye pulled into Hilltop, the reins the pilot held to control the train dragon were not directly attached to the reins on the dragon's girth strap. Otherwise, the dragon was so powerful that, with a twist, he could have pulled the pilot right out of his little box. The block and tackle pulleys inside the front of the box gave the pilot extra power.

I needed to work my way along the side of the train and get around to the front of the pilot's car as quickly as possible. The pilot's box had a small roof but the back was open. I swallowed and proceeded to crawl along the top of the car toward the pilot's box.

Within about ten feet of the box I crawled to the left edge, hoping to Heavens the pilot wouldn't look to that side. No curves ahead, so not likely. Still, I felt my heart in my throat until I eased myself over the edge of the car.

Below was another slat along the bottom edge of the wall. If I hung off the roof, there was a big gap from my feet down to the three-inch slat. It was too dangerous to drop down.

Dang it! On impulse, I headed for the back-left corner of the car roof instead. Once there, I reached for the ladder and worked my way down between the ladder and the side edge to rest my toes on the slat along the bottom of the wall.

Lucky for me, there were vertical slats and windows every four feet along the car's side walls. I guessed they were holding the wall's panels together. If this car had been built of rocks and mortar like every farm house around Hilltop, I could have simply gripped the rock edges to move along the wall, but... oh well.

Holding on to the back edge of the car, I reached for the first slat along the edge of the window and started working my way forward. The window was covered by heavy curtains so I would not be seen by anyone inside. Worked pretty well, but I kept an eye open for any bumps and curves on the tracks ahead.

Suddenly that became a very minor problem because at a glance back, I saw Clod with crossbow in hand, peering over the edge of the roof at me! Not the best place to whip out my slingshot and send a rock right between his eyes.

This is the end for sure. Now all he had to do was nail me with a bolt shot from his crossbow and I would be dead before I hit the hard ground rushing beside the train.

Was there a quick way forward before he could shoot? No, I was dead.

He lowered the crossbow toward me and fingered the trigger. I took one big step back and felt the bolt nick my left arm as it flew past.

"Dad-blamed lousy punk!"

Oh good, now he's really mad.

The smooth silvery surface of the tracks ahead changed to a section that was dark and rough looking, maybe marking a bump or bad rails.

I panicked and plastered myself against the wall of the car gripping the window on either side with a death grip. Fall and die. Stay put and get a sharp bolt through my ear—and die.

My face burned from friction against the rough wood as the car rocked side to side. I swear I heard the bow string hum a rising pitch as Clod pulled it back to notch it before the fatal shot.

Instead, the car lurched downward about an inch. I held on so tightly a shot of numbing pain ran through my fingers.

My body bounced away from the car's wall. The bones of my fingers nearly separated at the joints as I gripped harder. The wall receded from my face. I squeezed my eyes shut and waited for the bolt to pierce my head or for my body to slam into the ground below.

Nothing. Nothing but the wind blowing the hair in my face and the clickety-clack of the train wheels. I was still hanging onto the car. Hoping my hands wouldn't fail me, I looked up at Clod. Nobody there.

I pulled myself forward to hug the wall as I looked back at the tracks. A big ball of brown tunic and hair bounced down the slope from the tracks. Arms and legs swung crazy, unnatural ways. Clod's body crashed into a thicket of brush and rocks and seemed to explode in a cloud of dust and dark red blood.

I'd say that was the best two-for-one shot I would ever survive for the rest of my life. I apparently had a life left to live. At least for a few more minutes.

No time to dwell on what just happened, I stepped to the front corner of the car. At this angle I couldn't see the pilot. I began to edge around the corner. I realized I hadn't surveyed the reins to see how I had to disable them.

I crept back and looked at the reins. The best point of destruction was right at the bottom of the pilot's cabin where I could reach the reins from below. I couldn't reach where the thick straps of leather were threaded to the block and tackle system inside the pilot's box.

This was it. I couldn't just hang onto the car looking at the reins. I had to act. Now was as good a time as any. I started around the corner, keeping my eye on the cabin.

I was halfway to my goal when the face of the pilot turned toward me. At first, his expression was blank, then his face contorted into a combination of shock and anger.

"Hey, kid, what the blazes are you doing?" I heard his angry snarl above the roar of the wheels on the rails.

I rushed to my goal and crouched right below the front of the pilot's box. I grabbed onto the nearest rein and steadied myself on the wooden shaft. I reached in my pouch for my knife. I sawed on the rein, held tight by the raging pilot.

"What? Are you crazy? Do you want this train to crash? You stupid idiot!"

And on and on he went. Hearing a clattering noise above my head, I glanced up. The pilot was trying to grab the long dragon whip anchored on the side of the box so he could hit me with it. I sawed faster.

The leather was thick, tough, and well-tanned. For a moment I shuddered to think what kind of animal provided the leather. Was it a slaughtered dragon? I guess it didn't matter because I couldn't cut through it fast enough anyway. I would have to pull it out of the pilot's hands.

I felt the sting of his whip as it hit my head and shoulder. I struggled to hang on and didn't fall off the car. I couldn't take another one or two of those hits.

On impulse, I jerked hard on the rein and it suddenly loosened as the pilot lost his grip.

Above me, "What? How did you do that? Blasted little pile of dragon dung!"

He leaned way out of the cabin and grabbed the rein. Risking a quick death by losing my balance in front of the car, I pulled again on the rein as hard as I could. The pilot came with it. Instinctively I twisted to my left as the pilot still hanging on to the rein flew past me.

He hit the track with a dull thud and disappeared like a swatted fly.

Both reins were now loose.

My dad always complained I didn't have the guts to chop off a chicken's head, but I had probably ended the lives of two men. I wondered if Dad would approve or just think I was a murdering punk. My stomach turned and I threw up.

I tried to grab ahold of the reins and hoped I wasn't going to join the pilot plastered on the tracks behind the rushing train. I felt dizzy, on the verge of blacking out.

Suddenly the entire car lurched upward which helped me lean against the front of the car. I reached up to the empty pilot's box and gripped the edge of the front. My vision cleared.

I twisted my head around to see ahead. The train dragon flew upwards beyond his normal range. The reins that had controlled him whipped about uselessly. His harness restricting his wings and the shafts and straps of the attachment system didn't allow too much range of motion, but it was more than he was used to. He groaned loudly as he struggled to fly straight and not pull the train off the tracks.

A bigger disaster was about to happen because of the loosened dragon and the relentless momentum of the train behind him. Overhead, a huge blue streak appeared and then hovered above the dragon. It was Skye.

In my head I heard her firm but reassuring orders to the train dragon. *Be calm. Don't panic.*

What? the dragon said.

Skye answered, *Nothing bad is going to happen if you follow my directions. Fly straight, don't soar above. Don't worry about the reins. You're in control now.*

He glanced up. *Who are you? A free-flying dragon! Lord of the Dragons, what is this?*

Skye's words didn't seem to help the dragon right then, but they helped calm me. I needed to deal with the pilot's car as it dropped to its normal position. I adjusted my grip and stance to avoid falling off.

I pulled myself to the edge of the front and then clawed my way up to the box. With the car rolling more smoothly, I managed to pull myself in and collapse on the floor. Laying there for several seconds, I caught my breath and tried to ignore my aching body, especially my hands.

The train and the clickety-clack sound slowed.

I sat up and looked out.

Skye said to the train dragon, *Now back-flap so you can stop the train. We can't do anything else until you stop because the harnessing equipment is keeping you from being free.*

The dragon back-flapped as directed and the train slowed more.

Good, you've got a strong stroke. Skye looked back at me in the box. *Jaiden, pull on the brakes as I explained to you.*

I searched the pilot's box and saw two long levers emerging from the floor.

"I hope these are the brakes," I said to myself.

I pulled on them. Nothing. I pulled harder. Not much difference in speed.

I pulled with all the strength my aching body could manage and between the dragon and me, the train made a long, slow stop.

Skye landed in front of the train.

Come on, let's take care of the train dragon. We still have work to do.

EIGHTEEN

Free at Last!

I scrambled from the box and began unbuckling the backband on the train dragon to separate it from the girth and bellyband. I unbuckled the loin strap freeing the dragon from the long wooden shafts that hitched him to the pilot's car. Around front, I unchained the breast plate from the massive collar that circled the dragon's shoulders and neck. I was too small to attempt to remove the collar over his head.

With her mouth, Skye grabbed hold of the place where the reins slipped through rings at the top of its saddle and pulled the whole harness assembly off leaving only the collar on the dragon. She then removed the collar. I could see the train dragon take in a deep breath and shrug off not only the weight of the harness but the enslavement forced on him by the humans.

At that moment of victory, a horde of humans came around both sides of the front car.

Stay here, both of you, Skye ordered as she took to the air and flew south.

"Creator of the Heavens, she just flew off and left us here," I said.

Well, I can fly away, the dragon said. *Though I can't fly too well, it'll be much better without that evil harness on me.*

"It'll be all right and I could probably grab hold of your collar and hitch a ride, but Skye said to stay here."

Yes? the dragon said, sounding reluctant to stay while the humans approached, cursing loudly. *Skye, you say? I think that's Number 4, the escaped train dragon. I heard about her. There's talk all around the Big Barn in Portville. Of course, we don't let on to the humans about our rumors.*

"Yeah, you're right, that's her," I said. "Number 4 is Skye. She's never failed me or made an error in judgment. I know it's kind of scary, but couldn't you swing your head around, whip your tail at these madmen, and make a big enough fuss they would stay back... for a little while, anyway?"

I don't know. I've never challenged humans. I was raised in the stalls of Portville and the Dragon Train camps. I've only known fear of humans. But I don't like them one bit. He surveyed the crowd of men as they tightened in a semi-circle around us.

I had a sinking feeling they were going to quickly surround us.

"Do something! Now!" I ordered, a little surprised at my insistence and new-found authority.

With only the slightest pause, he did everything I suggested, uttering a terrifying roar that I never heard from Skye, and swinging his long snake-like body back and forth. I ran backwards barely fast enough to escape getting slammed by his tail.

The men's eyes opened like big fat bugs and nearly popped out of their heads. The front row was sent flying in all directions as the dragon flailed them right and left. Meanwhile, I was busy keeping my distance from his tail, as well as staying opposite of the crowd of men.

The crowd stampeded around to the sides of the train behind the front car.

"OK, stop!" I cried to the dragon. "They got the idea. Watch for anyone easing toward us or moving to the far left or right. Give them more of that same medicine if they dare come near."

The men heard my command and stayed put, although I could hear a few mutter, "What's he doing *talking* to a dragon like it understands? I mean they understand a little, kind of like a dog, but—"

This kind of talk wasn't good. How long could this standoff last? Surely the train's crew would know what to do with a berserk dragon.

I pulled out my sling and three rocks. I placed a rock in the sling's pouch, gripped the long leather cords and whirled it around a few times to make sure the rock was seated. I was ready for anyone who dared approach a boy who could send a rock between their eyes.

I worked my way to the edge of the crowd and glanced beyond the train. I couldn't see Skye anymore. What the blue blazes was she up to? What did she expect us to do on our own?

Then what looked like a little blue-tailed lizard flew toward us. I rubbed my eyes to clear my vision. She was carrying something. Something big and long.

A tree! She was bringing one of the trees we felled to block the train earlier. I marveled at her strength to carry a tree aloft, but what was she going to do with it?

Soon the cursing stopped. Complete silence settled in. I turned and saw the men transfixed by the same sight that awed me.

"That big blue dragon," the conductor said. "That's Number 4, the run-away from Hilltop! That dad-blamed stinking lousy no-good snake needs to be killed!"

Another crew member piped up, "I think that blue dragon is up to no good with that, that, whatever—Hades a'mighty she's going to kill us all! I don't get paid enough to hang around to get my brains smashed by a tree!"

A huge commotion arose faster than the speed of thought as the whole crowd scrambled to the back of the train. Some ventured several feet away from the train, but with only a few wispy trees in the distance, they stopped. They turned and ran back behind the tail end of the train.

Many cowered under the train cars. A great gaggle of cries and panicked shouting arose as Skye came within a hundred yards of us. She circled the entire length of the train, dipping her long wings nearly to the ground as she held the tree in her mouth like it was a loaf of brown bread.

Her voice filled my head. *Tell this crowd of cowards that I'll drop this tree on the train, time and time again until nothing is left of the train and all who hide inside. And those under it as well.*

I ran along the right side of the line of cars while whirling my sling and yelling again and again, "The Big Blue, old Number 4, is going to drop this tree on your stupid heads and cars until you're all dead!"

As I reached the end of the line, I ran up the other side repeating my warning. I sensed the resentment and evil thoughts as I rushed past.

No doubt, they were all thinking, *Who does this stupid punk kid think he is working as a lackey to that vile dragon?*

I heard muted but clear curses of "Traitor."

"Worthless brat."

"Why does he side with dragons?"

"That Number 4 shoulda been killed right off the bat! Now look at what the demon is doing!" and so on.

It bothered me to hear their curses, but I knew they didn't understand. They only had their prejudice and narrow-minded beliefs about the dragons to go on.

They didn't know Number 4 like I did.

I stopped near the front car and faced the muttering crowd glaring at me through the open windows and from underneath the cars.

Good, you got the point across, Skye said with a trace of pride I could sense. *Now tell all the humans to slowly move south away from the train. They are to keep walking until they reach the small trees in the distance. No one stays behind. If they don't obey... Well, you know.*

I announced as much to the crowd. Slowly as possible, men, women, and children moved away from the train, as I came around to the front and stood between them and the train dragon who remained in his position. Their faces and the muttering made it clear they resented a punk and dragons telling them what to do.

I conveyed the thought to the train dragon that he was to lunge at any people who acted like they were going to challenge Skye's orders. He came around to my right and gradually advanced towards the crowd as they retreated across the plains. Only a few tried to linger and get behind him.

They rushed to join the others as Skye swooped down and nearly knocked them off their feet with the tree and the wind from her wings.

Eventually the crowd was so far away, they looked more like spindly twigs growing along the Nulland horizon than people.

Skye landed near me as lightly as a barn owl. She dropped the tree and kicked up a cloud of dust.

There. Done with them. Now, Jaiden, you help get me hitched to the train. We're heading for Portville. You'll be the conductor—I don't need a pilot because I know where I'm going—and young man, she said to the dragon, *what's your name—not your number—but your name?*

Azul. I understand you're Skye.

The same. I'd love to visit but you need take your leave. Azul, enjoy your freedom.

But— Azul seemed at a loss for words. *I don't know. What are you two up to? Do you need help?*

I don't think so. Besides, two dragons towing a train might arouse a lot of suspicion. This is your chance to taste freedom.

But where do I go?

Skye thought a moment. *Head north. No, make that northeast. If you go straight north when you reach the mountain forests, you'll probably run into a group of under-handed gold dragons and maybe a silver dragon or two, who work for the humans. They were after us.*

Azul looked at me. *Oh yeah, I meant to ask. What's the deal with this human kid?*

No time to explain. But he's a friend. A very helpful and dear friend....

I was surprised and a bit embarrassed to hear myself described that way. Of course, it made me proud, but what would it mean to other humans? To my father? I was a traitor to humanity now. No way getting past it.

Oh well.

He and I have to rescue my family, once I discover where they are. She paused and looked at me with a look that was both amused and a little expectant. Like she wanted to be sure I was going with her to help.

"Of course," I said. "We're in this together." I turned to Azul, "You could help but I think Skye is right about two dragons and one train rolling into Portville. Too risky. And maybe word has already gotten there about us or at least Skye. So—"

OK, I get it. So, I travel northeast. Funny, I've never flown more than a few feet above the tracks, not open ground. I don't quite know how things look from there, but I guess I'll learn.

Skye nodded and said, *Don't veer too far east or you'll end up over the villages along the coast near Portville and then you'll be re-captured or killed especially once word of this 'Great Train Robbery' gets out.*

I'll be careful. But once I get past the forest to the north and the city to the east, then what?

I've heard there are free lands for dragons beyond. No idea of what it looks like or what kind of land to look for. Some rumors say desert. But it's a free desert.

Thanks, the young dragon said. *Good luck to you. I don't know how I can re-pay—*

Don't, Skye said. *Just be free and if you have a family someday, raise them to be free.*

Azul formed an expression very human-like as if he was about to cry with gratitude, but then he covered it with a determined look and took flight. Dang, I didn't know what to think about all this dragon emotion! We watched as he rose several yards above any elevation he had ever flown.

Skye said quietly, *He's scared but excited. I wish we could go with him. But I have family in Portville and we must get there on the chance that the humans won't hear the news of what's happened today until later.*

I helped her get hitched up. Good thing I hadn't cut the reins earlier. Still, it wasn't a very secure hitching because I didn't have the strength of dragon handlers. She felt it would do for the time being. I ran to the front car and found a closet inside with another conductor's red coat, black cap, and pants. I put the uniform on. To keep the cap from blowing off, I tucked it in the coat pocket as the train lurched forward.

I climbed into the pilot's box and, as a spectator only, watched the magnificent span of Skye's wings grab the air and propel us to—what?

Who knew? I was both excited to see the big city I'd always heard about and scared almost to unconsciousness wondering what would befall us.

NINETEEN

Country Boy in the Big City

I am lucky that great clouds of bugs weren't flying around the train as we left the Nulland Plains and entered Portville. My country boy's jaw dropped to the floor leaving my mouth wide-open to collect a mouthful of nasty insects. Just as the sun was setting behind us in the west, I took in the sights of a town way beyond anything I could imagine.

There were so many people walking to and fro, they reminded me of the hordes of locusts that attacked our field when I was a little kid.

Instead of our measly three streets that branched off the railroad through Hilltop, here were dozens of streets that stretched into the mists of dusk. And the buildings! Buildings, most five or more times taller than anything in my home town, lined the streets like beehives.

Soon our one set of train tracks joined several lines of tracks coming from and branching off in all directions. Other trains passed us coming and going. We blended in so well, no one seemed to notice when we approached a barn fifty times bigger than ours back home. Inside the gigantic entryway were countless station platforms where people were getting on and off trains.

Since we had only a few passenger cars but several cargo cars, no one looked twice as we continued to the loading docks along warehouses beyond the other end of the big barn-like building. Swallowing my uncertainty in spite of Skye's coaching for the last hour or so, I stepped off the landing of the front car, put on the conductor's cap and approached a man standing behind a tall box piled with fat books.

I cleared my throat as he continued to tick off items on an invoice. Trying to sound like an adult, I said, "Sir, I implore your assistance rounding up roustabouts to unload our cargo." I tried to look impatient and accustomed to this tiresome routine.

He scrutinized me as if I were a cockroach at his feet. "You're a little late. I've got more trains coming in." he said. "I should make you wait until morning."

"Please, uh, sir. We had to clear the tracks of some fallen trees..." I didn't like thinking so much on my feet. I waited a few tense moments.

He sighed. "Where are you coming from?"

Dang! I had no idea. What now? I tried to hold my expression steady trying to think of something—anything—to say.

Fortunately, Skye's thought entered my empty head. *Tell him, Clayhills.*

Weird name. But...

"Clayhills," I said. "You are expecting us, aren't you?"

He checked his pile of invoices. "Uh, let me see.... Hmm, I don't know—wait. Ah, here it is." He turned to a tall open door next to him and shouted into the darkness. "Charkley, bring a dozen of your men to unload the Clayhills train!"

A burly guy that looked old enough to be my grandpa but with muscles that rivaled my father's, came out with a bunch of young guys at his heels. They unloaded the train as the man behind the tall box checked off items.

I stood about trying to look bored while I sent off a thought of my own to Skye. *How did you know where this train came from? This could have been a disaster if you weren't right and this guy found his list didn't match the cargo.*

While you were busy with running off the passengers and crew back there on the plains, I questioned Azul about his train. It seems it always carries the same cargo this time of year. Mostly farm goods and some pottery because Clayhills is famous for its pottery crafts.

That was close, I thought. *What would we have done—*

You could have just told him anything. Once they started unloading cargo that didn't match the invoice, you could have gotten irate at his lack of a correct invoice.

Oh sure, make me the fall guy. I don't think I could have pulled it off.

Sure, you could. I have great confidence in you, Skye thought.

Never mind. They're done unloading. Let's move on before they realize I'm a fraud.

I boarded as Skye pulled the train ahead. Beyond the warehouse was another huge barn, this one for docking the train and unhitching the dragons to be taken to the stalls. Four men surrounded Skye and began releasing the harness, removing the collar, and other gear.

One of the men said, "Who rigged this dragon? It's too loose and some things weren't even attached properly." He turned to me, "Where's the pilot? I've got a lot of big bones to pick with the idiot!"

"Uh, the pilot... Well, he's not here. He wasn't feeling so good, so he left as we were unloading the cargo."

"What? How in the blue dragon blazes did you get the train here from the warehouse without a pilot?"

Oh, double dang! I spoke before I thought. "Well, he was bad sick so I took the reins coming here. This dragon's pretty cooperative, so it wasn't really a problem. Besides, I've had some pilot training."

The man looked at me skeptically. "Yeah, well, you should have a licensed pilot take the reins. There's usually one of the roustabouts who's qualified. I could report you to the guild. They don't allow non-pilots to take the reins, even a conductor. You know that."

"Sorry, I was so worried about the pilot. He's a close friend of the family and all...." Lord of the Heavens, how much longer was I supposed to shovel more of this bull manure?

"Humph! You're a bit wet behind the ears, young man, so I'll give you a pass for now. But don't expect any slack if *anything* like this happens again."

"Yes, sir, thank you." I clamped my mouth shut figuring I should quit while ahead.

But that chance only lasted another couple of minutes. As the crew finished unhitching Skye, the big blue threw a quick thought to me. *Don't forget. They can't take me to just any stall.*

Oh, triple dang! I almost forgot.

As the crew got a good grip on Skye's restraining lines, I called out. "Oh, yeah. I didn't mention before... We had a bit of a problem along the line several miles out. A big tree fell across the tracks and we used Sk—the dragon—to pull it off the road. We had to loosen some of her gear to do that. After moving that tree, the pilot said she had some injuries that needed looking at when we got here... Before she—it is taken off to the stalls."

The same man turned back and looked at me even more carefully. "Yeah? We didn't see anything wrong."

"Right, me too, but the pilot was pretty sure of it. He knows this dragon better than anyone. I think maybe he didn't get all the gear back on right because he was concerned about the injuries. He said the medics at the infirmary would know what to do. I honestly don't but I can take, uh, *it* to the medics to check out."

Again, a look from this guy. If he refused, I had no idea what I was going to do next.

"We don't have time to mess with this foolishness," the guy said. "I wish the pilot was here because this isn't something for me to deal with. I've got work to do. There's two dozen more trains coming in and it's almost quitting time."

"All the more reason you can just leave it to me. I'll take the dragon. What can it do now that it's surrounded by all these people who know a thing or two about dealing with trouble-makers? Besides this one is a pretty good dragon compared to most. I'll be fine...."

I don't know how confident I seemed to these men. I felt like a punk kid whose pants had just been pulled down by the school bully.

But somehow, I guess the combination of having a lot of work to do, wanting to go home to supper, and maybe—just maybe—a faint air of *seeming* like I knew what I was doing must have affected the head man. He nodded to me, motioned to his guys to hand two of the restraining lines and a long whip to me. Off they went back to the dock outside without one look behind.

Congratulations, Mr. Conductor, Skye said. *You're growing up fast especially compared to how you were just a few days ago in the forest outside Hilltop."*

"Oh, yeah, with those guys who came to take you away. I was messing in my pants, they had me so scared." I thought about it for a moment, and then finally took a deep breath. "I wasn't exactly calm and cool just now, but I guess I was trying to come off like I knew what I was doing."

And you do.

"Maybe. I've been around you long enough, so I feel like I know how to handle a big old blue dragon."

I sensed a dragon chuckle coming my way. *You know a little, but don't get too big for your britches.*

"Yes, ma'am." And I saluted her like I've seen people in Hilltop salute our postman since he was the closest thing we had to some kind of authority.

Careful, Skye cautioned. *You don't want any of these dragon handlers seeing you salute me.*

I whipped my hand to my side and we continued through the long aisle surrounded by dozens of stalls filled with dragons.

It's on ahead, through the giant door, Skye said. It was in front of us. I led her in.

Looking at it from the outside, I finally had a chance to take in the enormous barn, so big that its far walls disappeared in the dusty, humid air. There was certainly a barnyard smell to the place but I was used to that at home. Even though my dad and I had no dragons, we had horses, cows, and sheep which sure didn't smell much better.

As big as the barn looked from the outside, inside its size grew in my mind to bigger than the whole world. I looked to see not roof joists and planking but only a dark brown fog barely lit by the orange light of the numerous oil lamps hung on every other post along the endless line of stalls. Perhaps in the daylight I would see the true extent of the building and the details of the ceiling.

We walked along slowly as stall boys were rushing about pulling wagons of hay, hauling off manure, and a few men taking other dragons to their stalls. *Come on,* I urged Sky. *I'm afraid I'm still going to get caught pretending to be a conductor.*

Settle down. If you look frantic, that will draw attention.

OK, OK. I forced myself to walk slow and hoped my face was blank.

We came to an intersection. *Turn left here,* Skye commanded. *Only a few yards ahead, I think.*

"The infirmary?"

No, my family. Caerulus was a train dragon like me, but the children—I just don't know. They may have kept them with him or not. When I was last here— She couldn't go on, even to complete the thought in her mind. *Let's just go and see.*

"But if they're not here, then what?"

I don't know. Maybe back to a training camp. Maybe the slaughterhouse— No! I can't think that way. Not yet. Just keep going. At the next intersection, turn right.

I looked around as we walked on. No one really paid attention to one young conductor leading a big blue. So, I guess it wasn't so unusual after all. And I did see a few stalls that had one or two adult dragons with younger ones.

Maybe, just maybe Skye's family was still here.

We came to the intersection. Skye stopped. Her huge lungs blew air stirring straw and dust from the ground. Then she took a long, slow breath. *OK, continue,* she said quietly.

We turned and she slowed her pace. Passing scattered wagons and carts, I looked around for a single adult dragon and three youngsters in a stall. Then I saw them just ahead on our right.

But something was wrong. Alongside the stall's gate was a large wagon, or should I say, a cage of metal bars on wheels big enough to hold a dragon family. Two handlers huddled near the wagon in a hushed conversation.

Caerulus! My babies! Oh, Demon of the Dragons, they might be preparing to take them away right in front of my eyes!

Suddenly I felt like I should be the motherly one. "Calm down. Don't show those handlers you care. Look, there's a stall right across from them that's empty. Let's take a chance and I'll put you in there."

But what if the real occupant comes along?

"We'll think of something when the time comes. You're cunning enough. Just go in. Don't make eye contact with Caerulus or he might tip the men off by his reaction. We can't do anything now because we're too deep into this dragon barn."

OK, OK, you're right.

We strolled into the stall like we belonged there. At least, like Skye belonged. I fiddled around with her restraining lines untying them. Finally, I got her all the way in beyond the tiny corral between the gate and into the actual stall. It was like one for a horse, though ten times bigger.

Through the gaps between the slats of the stall, I took a close look at the two men still standing by the wagon. I didn't think either had noticed us. I removed my conductor's cap and peeled off the coat and trousers. Underneath, I had on my regular clothes. If anything, I could pose as a stall boy coming to water the dragon and scoop some giant poop piles.

Nearly an hour went by while the men occasionally walked closer to Caerulus' stall, stared at him and the children, then walked back looking long and hard up and down the wide aisle. By that time, most of the stall workers had left and no more handlers came by.

Finally, the men by the wagon left.

Skye started breathing normally again. *Maybe they changed their minds because the other handlers might be gone for the night and there's no one to help them. It'll take at least ten men to move my family.* Then she shifted on her feet as if the ground was burning. *I don't know. I think they will find someone and come back tonight. Those kinds of wagons are not normally parked in the dragons' barn for nothing.*

"We don't have much time to waste," I said. "See if you can contact Caerulus and let him know—"

No. I'm not sure if he could sense my thoughts from this distance. He's not expecting me and even if he could sense me, he might act before thinking. It's too risky.

"All right. Then give me something to tell Caerulus that will convince him I'm a friend of yours because I'm going there now. Coming from me might give him a chance to think twice and not lose control. Or not, I don't know."

You're right.

She told me what to say. I was rather stunned... but, oh well. I walked to Caerulus' stall.

My natural fear of dragons grew and overwhelmed me. Skye was one thing but this Caerulus even at several yards away was much bigger than her, and he looked mad enough to chew railroad tracks. And me, too!

Caerulus paced inside the stall, murmuring something to the young ones. He entered to the corral and looked all around. Then he looked at me through the iron gate.

Oh, dragon manure.

I tried to swallow my fear so I could at least talk. "Hey there, big guy. How's it going?"

I felt his anger like the heat from a horseshoe right out of the forge.

Strangely enough, he didn't say or think anything. But the emotion almost knocked me down.

I tried again, only this time I conversed with my thoughts. *Look, I know you can understand and hear my thoughts. And I can hear your thoughts if you want me to. Hang on, I'm going to tell you something surprising. Don't let on you understand me because someone might notice. I am a friend of Skye.*

I watched him. His eyes brightened as the slits of his pupils widened, pushing the golden irises to the very edge of his eyes. Other than that, there was no reaction but quickened breathing.

I really know Skye, and she has sent me here to help you and the children escape, I thought with as much firmness as I could manage. *This caged wagon is not here for decoration and those two handlers are looking for help to load you as I speak.*

The slits of his pupils narrowed. If he could have made fire in this throat, I would have been a charred piece of meat. But he only glared, so I remained looking at him with what I hoped was self-assurance.

Prove it, the simple thought came to me in a very manly way.

I figured as much and I don't blame you for not trusting a farm boy. So, here's the deal. Don't get mad at me because this next thing I'm going to pass on to you comes from Skye.

I paused for effect, hoping Caerulus remained calm. And then I thought....

She said that, 'Your Sweet Snuckcums sends her love.'

His face transformed from something like shock to dumbfoundedness to white-faced anger—this on the face of a blue dragon! And finally, thank the Creator, an expression of sad sweetness, which I didn't think his face was capable of forming.

It must be true! You have to be a very special friend because she would not share that name with anyone. Even our children. It is our most private secret....

He paused. A bit of the former anger returned to his face, and I heard his thought, *So, what is it that brings her to such desperation?*

She is nearby. Don't look! Don't take your eyes off me. We have come to rescue you and the children as quickly as possible.

His reply didn't sound so friendly. *You are both insane. How can—*

Don't argue. We'll figure it out. All of us, not just her, not just me. Are you ready?

I heard nothing and I could tell by his face it was because he couldn't think of a thing to say. Then....

OK. It's insane, but I'm afraid we're bound for the knackers so they can cut us into steaks to feed to their worthless gold and silver traitors. Sure, the humans trained me and ran me on many routes. But I think I'm probably too big for some pilots to handle on a cross-country run. And so...

All right, I thought. *Glad to hear we're just in time. Again, don't look, but she's across the aisle from you a little to your right.*

He glanced briefly only with his eyes. I could sense her stare coming across the distance between them. In his eyes I saw a transformation into the kind of softness that I imagined was not unlike the look my parents, in their youth, may have exchanged.

Enough of that, I interjected. *Down to business. Feel free to interrupt if you have better ideas. But here's Skye's plan for all of us to escape before dawn....*

TWENTY

Best Laid Plans of Dragons and Men

Caerulus lifted his monstrous head and looked at me. Was this when he would raise a mighty front leg and squash me like a tomato hornworm? The way my father made me do every summer when the plants produced their tiny green tomatoes?

He nodded his head slightly and didn't squash me.

Good simple plan. It might work if we can get some human help. You were right when you thought there could be some like yourself who aren't pleased with what humans do to dragons.

Oh, good. Where do I find these people?

Right here among us. Mostly those who muck the stalls. I don't imagine any young men like scooping up all kinds of manure, especially the piles dragons can dump! He smiled so evilly that if I hadn't known the whole thought behind that expression, it would have filled me with fear.

Looking around, he leaned close to me as if to whisper in my ear. *In two stalls down from my beloved's are three boys who have often complained fiercely about their cruel bosses, the terrible jobs they have, and their reluctant admiration of dragons. I think they're romantics who imagine themselves riding dragons into battle.*

I smiled, remembering my own fantasies as a boy growing up in boring little Hilltop mucking manure in my father's barn. It had not occurred to me before but my fanciful imagination may have been the very reason I ran down to the station to view Skye collapsed on the tracks. And why I was sympathetic to her cause.

If there is a fourth boy with the three others, Caerulus said, *then say or do nothing. But the three always stick together, so be open with them quickly. Time will run out very soon.*

He gave me a look much like my father's when he was making himself very clear.

Got it. I'll be back if all goes well.

I sauntered to the indicated stall. I saw three guys a little younger than me scooping dragon poop into a huge wheelbarrow. As I walked up to them ready to make my proposal, a fourth boy appeared carrying a pitchfork. Dang it, now who is who?

"Something you want, sir?" the taller of the three at the wheelbarrow asked me.

"Uh, no. I just, I was looking for a, uh, handler. I need to move Caerulus—I mean, the big guy at that stall," I said pointing in Caerulus' general direction.

The tall boy looked along the aisle directly at Caerulus. "Yeah? Caerulus, huh?" he said with a bright look in his eyes.

Was that what he was waiting to hear from me, a name for a dragon who would normally be nameless to humans?

"Yeah," I said. "He needs some work done on his harness. Had a problem the last time he towed a train."

"You're looking in the wrong place," the same boy responded. He glanced at the one carrying the pitchfork. "Hey, Meremoth, you call that hay good enough for a train dragon?"

"What?" Meremoth said.

"I don't know where you got that stuff from, but it's not for the beasts who actually work." His voice gained an edge that matched the disdain on his face. "It's OK for their vermin children, but not for those who have to flap their wings for hours on end. Go back to the grain bins and bring the special oats, barley, and molasses mash our big guys need."

"Sorry. I'll go right now. What do I do with this load of straw?" he said as he pointed to a cart loaded with hay.

"Take it there for the little ones staying with the big blue," the tall boy said as he pointed right at Caerulus' stall.

"Yes, sir. Right away." The boy picked up the tow shaft and pulled the cart down the aisle.

The tall boy looked at me and smiled. "You said the magic word, guy. Now before you tell me what *Caerulus* needs, I'm called Altan." He shook my hand. "What about you?"

"Jaiden." I smiled. At that point, I think he realized I wasn't much older than him.

"Good name." He turned to the other two and pointed to one, then the other. "This guy here with the copper-colored hair is Mamun and blue-eyes is Fitzwater."

"Glad to meet any fellow humans who are friends of dragons."

I explained our get-away plan to Altan, Mamun and Fitzwater. Their excitement grew and I had to hold them back from running right to Caerulus' stall and get the family ready to escape.

"First, we have to reunite him and his mate," I said. "She's in the stall right across from him."

"Mate? Wow!" Mamun said. "This will be an adventure worthy of the retelling."

"Maybe so," I said. "But not today or any time soon. Come on."

We returned to Caerulus just as Meremoth tossed his pitchfork in the back of his empty wagon and began towing it away to the far back end of the dragon barn. The boys quickly conferred with the big dragon while I rushed to Skye with the news.

The first signs of real joy and energy showed on her face since I found her lying on the tracks in Hilltop.

It's going to work! she said. *I just know it. I had almost given up all hope when we came here. I couldn't imagine how we could find anyone among the humans working here who felt like you. But now I know my mate and I must have one more thing in common. We know how to find good human beings!*

I was flattered but still a little skeptical of these three boys. Would they really betray their fellow humans to help dragons? But it seemed they could also communicate with Caerulus and dragons like I could.

With her restraining lines in hand, I escorted Skye across the wide aisle to her family. Inside the stall away from prying eyes, they exclaimed their joy in thoughts I couldn't understand. Must be dragon language no human would know.

Skye and Caerulus were quite happy and maybe a bit embarrassed to show it in front of four young guys. They wrapped their long necks around each other and rocked back and forth for a few minutes. The children ran around their parents' legs and kicked up their feet, flapping their stunted wings in joy.

I don't know about the other three boys, but seeing Skye and Caerulus in their dragon hug and the children dancing about brought a lump into my throat I didn't expect. Finally, I had to take matters in hand.

"I know we're all pretty happy right now. But we're still within this big dragon barn and there's no freedom for any of us if we are caught."

Yes, of course, Skye said. *There will be time for more joy later. Let's get to work.*

The four of us helped Caerulus get outfitted with his harness and then Mamun and Fitzwater strapped the children with small harnesses to secure them to the caged wagon. Altan helped me with Skye.

We loaded her on the wagon and attached her lines loosely to the bars of the cage. Then the children were placed at her feet in such a way to seem they were secured. Last, we belted the girth connecting the shafts at the front of the wagon to Caerulus' harness.

I pulled my coat back on and advised the boys to get theirs.

"Why?" Altan asked.

"I'll explain later," I said. "Just get them now."

The smaller boys walked behind the wagon while Altan and I walked ahead of Caerulus as if we were leading him.

Without looking at Altan, I said, "I'm not sure what we are going to say if anyone challenges us about this strange procession."

"Don't worry about it. I've worked in this barn for three years already. I've seen just about everything, so I've a story to tell if anyone gets suspicious."

"Good. I'll leave that to you then." I looked at him sideways. I figured him to be no more than thirteen years old, yet he carried himself like someone at least two years older than me.

"So, what are you doing here if you don't like what's going on?" I asked.

"The three of us come from a village where we're the poorest of the poor. My family has no land of their own, hardly a garden with a few potatoes, corn and a scrawny milk cow on loan from one of the few landowners in town.

"The only chance our families have is for us to work here in the barns and have the train company send them our pay, small as it is. We'll just head back home after a few years of hard work. The train company likes their workers young, strong, and ignorant. They send our families half of what we make. The rest is kept by the bosses for 'expenses' like the gruel they feed us—not near as good as the mash they feed the dragons—and our rooms. Cold, infested with rats, and straw for mattresses."

"Still, why help us?" I wondered aloud.

"No choice. If our families could only buy an acre or two of land, we would have a chance to take care of ourselves." He spit and I could tell he considered what he would say next. "Maybe we stay on here and work our way to dragon handler, or conductor, or even pilot, though most of our kind don't make it that far. But they keep hiring more kids and men, maybe there's a chance for us scum to make it."

Altan grew silent.

"But...." I goaded him to say more.

"I couldn't stand being mean to dragons," he said without a pause. "Those big guys and gals are better than most people once you understand them. My buddies feel the same way, but we have to be careful. Most guys, like that little butt-kissing Meremoth, have a better chance because his family comes from an important town and they have connections. This is just a stepping stone for him to become a big boss."

I mulled that over for a little while, but ahead of us was the open door to the outside. We had to tend to the business at hand.

"Let's fall back and walk with Mamun and Fitzwater," I said to Altan.

As the four of us walked, I explained about how to safely ride a dragon.

"You mean we don't get to ride right on top like we would a horse?" Mamun asked.

"That's right. The last thing you want to do is get blown off especially if your dragon needs to move around and change direction suddenly. You'll be all right. The view will distract you from any stupid concerns."

Skye interjected into our conversation, *Listen to Jaiden, he's flown on me quite a distance since last week. We promise we'll get you home before they know what we've done here this morning, but you may have to leave your homes if they discover you had anything to do with our escape.*

Altan laughed. "They could care less where we come from, but they will keep an eye out for us. We'll never be able to go back to work here, for sure. Best chance we'll have is to find a job with some farmer in our village who has more land."

The other two boys piped in with their assurances.

We stopped just inside the barn as we approached the outside door. In the shadows, Mamun and Fitzwater got the young ones out of the cage. Altan and I helped Skye and Caerulus get their wing hobbles all the way off. I tightened their harnesses so we could hang on to them when we all took flight.

"Hey, you punks, just a gall-darned minute! Who told you to take the hobbles off those slimy dragons? Stop it right now or I'll slam the whole bunch of you into a pile of lizard manure!" The voice behind me sent fear deep into my bowels. I turned and there stood a big guy holding a pitchfork. I swore it was Clod, the guy in the Emerald Forest who then tried to kill me on the train. But he ended up getting killed or at least severely injured! This couldn't be the same guy. Clod's twin?

As he approached us, he swung the pitchfork and pointed it at me. One good lunge and he could send it through my throat. Getting eye contact with me, he stiffened and looked confused.

"Wait a minute." He growled. "What's a *conductor* doing releasing these beasts with the help of a bunch of stall boys? What is this?"

My mouth went limp and my brain froze. What could I say? I waited for something from Skye. I turned to look at her in desperation. All she did was gather her children close to her by wrapping her wings around them. Caerulus stepped toward the big guy.

Oh, Great Creator, I thought. *Are we going to have a fight right here in the barn before we escape?*

Skye grasped Caerulus with her wing.

No. Wait, my brave one. If we start a big fight, every human in the barn will rush us. We have to quiet him down.

I turned away from the dragons and scanned the area around us. I didn't see anyone yet. But then a couple of stall boys came out of a nearby corral and looked our way.

Without thinking, I stepped toward this Clod-looking guy and started talking with no idea what I was going to say until it left my lips. "No. Calm down, please. This isn't what you think."

"Oh yeah, you brainless moron! What do you suppose I think when I see a bunch of stall boys and a stupid looking conductor taking hobbles off dragons and releasing them from their cage? Is this just a little picnic with your dragon friends?"

He aimed the pitchfork and threatened to thrust the long, sharp prongs through my chest. Instinctively, I guessed what Caerulus would do in response. To avoid a big commotion, I raised a hand signaling the big blue to stand down. I wanted to handle this.

I grabbed a handful of straw and tossed it into the man's face. He raised the pitchfork to block his face from the cloud of straw and dust. I sprung and pushed him hard.

He took a step back, enough to allow the three boys and Caerulus to rush forward and help me bring the guy down. I grabbed more straw and attempted to jam it into his mouth. At that moment, Caerulus swept me aside and head-butted the man, knocking him senseless. And he did it without raising much more than the sound of a few scuffling feet.

Oh well. I turned to smile at Caerulus and thank him for backing me up. But before I could say anything, Skye's thoughts poured into my head.

No time to celebrate. Keep it quiet. Though I wasn't much help, I took a quick look around and I see handlers approaching. At least the stable boys nearby ran back into their stall without a sound once they saw you and Caerulus knock this man down. I think they're scared they'll be next.

"Let's leave now while we still have a chance," I whispered to the boys and dragons.

"Not yet," Altan said. "I'll cover this guy with a lot of straw while you go on out. I'll follow as soon as I can. Go!"

Not having any better idea, I motioned to the rest to get out the door.

Both Skye and Caerulus quickly picked up their children by gripping their harnesses in their mouths. Skye held one while Caerulus had two. I marveled how those big beasts with all their teeth could somehow hold their children without dropping or hurting them.

I climbed on Skye with Fitzwater on the other side of her harness. He was smaller than the other two boys and we didn't want to overload her. Altan ran through the wide door and joined Mamun on the opposite side of Caerulus.

Dawn hadn't broken yet as we faced open countryside to the east. Both dragons flapped their wings and began a brisk run straight ahead toward fields of grain barely visible in the darkness. They lifted their legs and continued building speed, then Caerulus angled upward while Skye followed.

I looked behind us and hoped with all my heart that a bunch of men didn't run out the barn to see us take off. So far, so good!

To the east, I saw a wide river pour into what appeared to be a lake that stretched into the mist beyond sight. Was that the Great Sea I had heard stories about? The size of the river and the sea was so far beyond anything I had seen around Hilltop. Then it disappeared.

We climbed quickly into low-lying clouds. It was so cold, it felt like a thousand pins pierced every square inch of my skin that wasn't covered. I gritted my teeth and bore it. We had to get out of sight of the barn and Portville before the dragons could fly lower where it wasn't as cold.

I said to Skye, *I don't know what's going to happen when that big lunkhead comes to. I couldn't see those other handlers after we were airborne. They may have seen us. This is going to make life difficult for all of us—*

Any worse than it already is? she said. *It would have only been a few minutes before they discovered our absence and not much longer to realize who helped us escape anyway. But I do worry for these boys.*

I hadn't thought of that. *Of course. I guess they may not be able to return home because that lunkhead and the dragon trainers will know exactly who helped us.*

It wasn't the time for a talk with the boys, so I kept it to myself as we flew.

Finally, after what seemed to be hours of agony, the dragons glided downward heading northeast as the sun rose and the warm updrafts from the fields brought comfort. At least, more comfortable than the frigid heights.

The fields gave way to barren land riddled with rocks and a few small streams. As some clumps of oak and elm trees appeared among small hills and valleys, the land became greener, but not as lush as it was around Hilltop. Soon, we flew above a few small farms.

Caerulus, land somewhere away from these farms, Skye said.

They landed. I gathered the boys together. "Guys, we made your lives a lot more dangerous back there and—"

"Don't worry about it," Altan said. "Right, guys?" he said to Mamun and Fitzwater.

Fitzwater nodded and Mamun said, "Yeah, those men were always kicking our butts about something, so they're probably not surprised we took off. It happens all the time."

"But what's different," Altan added, "is that low-lifes like us don't help dragons escape and take off with them." He looked seriously at me but then smiled. "We'll be fine. A lot of people in our village hate the train people like we do. We just don't have much choice when it comes to getting some kind of job that pays good but demands we do things we hate. You would be surprised how many in our families and neighbors hate what they do to the dragons."

Caerulus smiled and nodded to the boys. It was clear there was a friendly relationship between these boys and the big dragon.

"All right," I said. "I guess that's that for now. Let's get all of you home as quick as possible."

We dropped off the two younger boys at an isolated location where they could walk a few miles to their homes.

"Be careful," I said to Mamun.

He nodded in agreement. "Bye."

Both waved at the dragons while Fitzwater said, "We just want to be free, too."

"We promise to keep low in our neighborhoods," Mamun said, "if by wild chance, the train security men came looking for us."

As we rose into the sky, the two boys waved from the ground, smiling bashfully.

Altan was the last one to be dropped off by Caerulus. I climbed off Skye and walked over. We readjusted the harnesses on both dragons now that they no longer had a load of human boys. The young dragons wandered around for a few minutes while I faced Altan.

"Good luck," I said. "You've been a great help. If fate allows, I'll return to this little valley and check on you and the other guys someday. If I can, I'll bring something to make all this worthwhile. Without you and your friends, we would still be trying to hide in that barn."

"We'll be fine," he said. "I was tired of the work and feeling like I was a chump for staying under those conditions. If they come and take all the money from my family that I earned or even throw me in jail, it will still be worth it. Dragons gotta fly free and I hope I can live free myself someday."

"You will. We all will. Bye and take care," I said. I felt a wad of emotion threaten to choke me up, but I managed to hold it in until I could laugh and give Altan a good-natured punch.

He punched back and gripped my hand stronger than I expected. Altan went and said goodbye to Caerulus. The big dragon nodded his head to the boy but said little to him through his thoughts.

I guessed I was the only privileged human to "talk" a lot with dragons.

I climbed back on Skye and we headed north for a distant, rocky hill where the dragons could stop for a long-deserved rest before we planned what to do next.

I slept off and on during the afternoon, night, and the following morning. But Skye and Caerulus slept straight through except for a few half-asleep grouchy mutterings when the children got rambunctious and wanted to play "King of the Mountain" by climbing on their parents. I just laughed but finally herded the little ones away to play on the back side of the hill while I watched them.

The dragon children might be "little ones" but the oldest male, Baldric, was bigger and heavier than me. Deryn, the female was about the size of a calf and the youngest male, Jarmil, was as big as a shepherd dog. The amount of energy they possessed was something on the order of six-month-old pups.

By night time, I was exhausted and finally got grouchier than Caerulus and Skye and yelled, "Get to bed, or curl up somewhere and go to sleep! You're driving me crazier than you did your mom and dad! If you don't, I swear I'll tie all three of you together."

They apparently didn't understand human language or thought because all I heard from them was some grunting and whining, sounding something like my old dog. The three of them could take me down, but my manner startled them enough for them to lay down, stretch their legs, and go to sleep within two minutes.

Why didn't I put my foot down before?

Serenaded by a chorus of two grown and three juvenile snoring dragons, my eyelids got heavy after a skimpy supper of dried meat and hard bread I found in my conductor's coat. I guess he had that in reserve for a quick bite to eat if he was too rushed for a regular lunch.

Goodnight dragons, one and all. No sleep in the last two days... let's see what a new day brings.

TWENTY-ONE

The Circle Shall be Unbroken

Ohhhh! The new day brought *pain*. One solid lump of pain from the top of my head to the tips of my toes and fingers with no relief in between. I hadn't done all the heavy lifting like Skye and, later, Caerulus did. But I was done in by all that crawling along the top and sides of the train, dragging limbs and branches, manning whips and restraining lines, fighting, hanging onto Skye's harness while in flight... Creator of Heaven, I hurt!

I would have thought a farmer boy like me could handle any physical labor as if it were nothing, but obviously not.

On the other hand, the little dragons were already tussling quietly among themselves so as not to awaken a grumpy human. Skye was awake soaking in the warmth of the rising sun while Caerulus was nowhere to be seen. Did I dream him up in my delirium yesterday?

No, a flying blue lizard came toward us from the east. He appeared to be carrying something. Breakfast?

He landed smoothly. He strutted around like a regal lord of air and land as he sauntered to Skye and me.

It feels so good to have that wing harness off. I didn't appreciate my new freedom yesterday in our haste to escape and return our friends to their homes. But now—I feel freer than I ever felt before. I wasn't born in freedom like you, my love, he said to Skye.

I'm so glad for you, she said. *What have you brought for us?*

He dropped a limp hog in front of us.

This should do all of us for breakfast, don't you think?

I was hungry. Quite hungry. Ready to have that entire hog to myself. But I really liked such meat well-done. I didn't know what to say. Should I get picky or whiny? Or grit my teeth and dig in without complaint and hope my stomach wouldn't cast off raw meat like a rotten corpse—which it wasn't because it was still warm and fresh—what do I do?

Skye read me like a book. She turned to Caerulus and nudged his neck with the top of her head as she said to him, *Flame of my heart, I think we might prepare that like the humans do and how blues have traditionally done. You know, cook it.*

What? he looked at his mate as if wondering what she was thinking. *I don't—oh. Yes, I agree. Pardon my manners, I'm not used to human company beyond those boys in the barn. They always had their own food.*

Skye turned to me. *Do you think you can start a fire somehow?*

"Oh sure, done it many times when I camped on the meadows herding sheep." I scrounged around the rocks at our feet and found a couple of extra hard stones and a handful of dry grass.

"Skye, could you find a few pieces of wood somewhere around here?" I asked.

Without a word she wandered down the side of the hill. In my earlier search through the conductor's pockets, I found a metal blade with a rough strip on one side used, no doubt, to light a pipe for a relaxing smoke. Apparently, he or I lost the other piece which had a coating to create a spark. Looking around, I found a good rock that would do the trick.

I rubbed the dry grass vigorously to pulverize it as much as possible. Caerulus and the little ones gathered around, curious about what this human was up to. Skye came back with a nice collection of kindling and a thick branch that she broke into several pieces with her front foot.

After I made a few well-aimed strikes of rock against metal, the sparks got the grass to smoking. I blew into the smoke, making burning embers brighten. Once I saw flames, I piled on the small kindling and then the larger pieces as the fire grew.

Caerulus and the children laughed.

Caerulus said, *I've seen fires around the human quarters in the barn and the training camps, but we've never seen how they started a fire. Rather sad for a dragon to admit.*

Gathered around the fire, they almost got in my way as I placed a few big rocks surrounding the wood to support the hog. I trimmed a thick stick to use as a fork. I could then turn the hog to cook a portion of the loin for a high-on-the-hog hunk of pork for breakfast. Once I had something I was satisfied with, I carved off my piece of meat with the conductor's blade.

"Have at it, folks. I've got my cooked piece. Just don't burn yourselves."

There a long pause of silence, Caerulus started to chuckle and then Skye. After their mother explained the joke I made when I told the dragons, "don't burn yourselves," Baldric, Deryn, and Jarmil finally joined in the laughter. It was one of the tastiest and most pleasant meals I've ever had even if the pork lacked a sprinkling of salt and chile to make it ideal.

Stomachs full, heads clear, bodies refreshed, we took to the air heading north again. I wasn't sure what Skye had in mind, but she was in the lead so I said nothing.

The air had warmed considerably and I felt like a morning nap as the rhythmic flow of Skye's wings lulled me to dozing.

Suddenly there was a cry of alarm from two dragon minds.

I awoke with such a start I almost fell off Skye.

Golds! Silvers! Fast approaching from behind! Caerulus roared in my mind. If he had yelled out loud, it would have pierced my ears.

In no time, four golden and three silver dragons with gold riders flew all around us! Skye pleaded to Caerulus, *Down, my love! Quickly, before they cross under us and we're trapped.*

Skye and Caerulus dropped lower. Skye's sudden drop toward the ground almost made me throw up my wonderful breakfast. I clamped my jaw shut, gripped my stomach with my free hand, and willed my breakfast to stay put.

I could feel Skye's powerful muscles pulse, elongate, and contract violently as she reached high above her back, flapped harder, and rotated her wings farther back and down. She flew faster than I had ever witnessed before. Caerulus followed close behind. The wind gusting hard in my ears, I looked back and saw the other dragons recede far behind us.

We soared only a few feet above the ground, rising and dropping to follow the hilly terrain. The dragons found an abandoned farm in a deep narrow canyon where a stream once flowed.

Skye and Caerulus landed and dropped the children to the ground beside a dilapidated barn. I glanced to see the sky was empty. We had lost them!

Run, my little ones! Into the barn, Skye said.

Hurry! Caerulus' more insistent voice ordered. The children quickly dashed into the barn.

Off, Jaiden, Skye ordered. *You won't be able to hold on and will be in danger if you stay on me. We'll return to get all of you when we're done.*

"But—"

No! No argument. Off! She shook herself hard and I fell off like a pesky fly. *Run! Into the barn!*

I ran.

The young dragons followed right behind me.

Close the door and go to the far corner. Hide yourselves as best as possible and stay there until we're back, Skye said.

I ushered the young ones into a manger, closed the gate behind me, and peeked through twisted slats in the wall to watch Skye and Caerulus have a kind of war council just outside the open barn door. The two of them put their heads together as she brought something out of the saddle bag in her harness to give to Caerulus.

What did she have in that saddle bag?

Caerulus became restless and made odd sounds that seemed excited to me. She quieted him. Though I could sense thoughts coming from them, it was that unintelligible dragon language again. They rushed out of sight as Skye closed the rickety door behind them and with loud flapping and two whooshes of wind, they were gone.

I ran across the barn and burst through the door, knocking it completely off its hinges.

"What in the Blue Dragon Blazes are you doing? Are you crazy?" I yelled at the receding sight of two lizards flying into the mist above.

Skye's fading voice whispered to me, *We can't outrun them for much longer. We have no choice!*

So, it's come to this, I thought to myself as I turned toward the barn. The children, wide-eyed, eased their way out of the barn. I shooed them back in, but they weren't easily persuaded. What if I ended up with these three permanently? How does one take care of three young dragons?

"Go, dad-blame it! I don't want to be your nursemaid any longer than necessary. And I sure don't want your mother mad at me for letting you all out in the open. Back!"

They believed me and faded into the darkness of the decrepit barn.

I heard a strange sound, something like the hiss of snakes—snakes the size of a house. I looked up. A knot of small dragons with gaping mouths, weaved around Skye and Caerulus. This wasn't going to be pretty.

The four gold dragons which were not mounted on silvers, darted around like crazed bats. The silver dragons, ridden by golds, spewed skimpy bursts of fire at the blue pair. I was stunned to see how well Skye danced about more adeptly than seemed possible for her size. Caerulus wasn't as agile but his size made up for it. When he lunged at the smaller dragons, they scattered.

The silvers' fire wasn't far reaching. This confirmed what Skye had told me about the humans cutting back their power. Had the humans performed some kind of surgery to shrink the size of their throat packs of sulfur to prevent the silvers from turning their fire against their captors?

One of the free-flying golds dipped and attacked with quick swipes and short bursts of flame. It certainly irritated but did not slow down Skye and Caerulus. The blue pair circled wide to avoid the flames and swung their massive heads at the other dragons. But the golds and silvers were too agile to get hit.

Skye and Caerulus then flew toward each other. The golds chortling in glee as they flew in a circle around the blues. As the circle tightened, a silver, at the commands of its rider, dipped underneath the blue pair while a second silver wound in a tight spiral above them. The two silvers closed in slowly, squeezing the blues between them. The third silver and its gold rider flew off several hundred yards to the west and glided back and forth as if waiting to ambush Skye and Caerulus.

Allowing the silver pair to close in more, the free-flying gold dragons sped around the perimeter. They fanned out to form a sphere around the silvers and blues and then, they too, tightened the sphere.

Skye called to Caerulus, *Now!*

As they rotated back-to-back facing the closing sphere of dragons around them, both took in deep breaths, elongated their necks and opened their mouths wide. An array of long sharp teeth glinted in the sunlight. Next, both closed their mouths followed by a quick snap open.

Their teeth clashed together and sparks flew out of their mouths.

"What?" I said. Then came the realization. "Oh, wow! Oh, wow! This is gonna be—"

TWENTY-TWO

Well-Placed Rocks

A whoosh filled the air as if a sudden tornado blew into the narrow canyon. Caerulus' and Skye's mouths spewed a slender stream of yellow and red flame. Then the spray burst into a pulsing column of fire from Skye and Caerulus when they aimed at each of the two closer silver dragons and their riders.

A wall of wind hit me like a horse that had just run me down. Slammed on my back, my vision blurred for several moments. As my sight came back, I saw the silvers and golds were stunned for a moment too long before they fired back in answer to the blasts that enveloped them.

I felt the urge to pull out my sling and arm it with two rocks. It wasn't the usual thing to do since two rocks could become unbalanced in the sling's pouch and fly off in the wrong directions. But it had worked once before when I brought down a big groundhog on the farm last spring. I took a chance and loaded both in my sling.

But it was too late for the two mounted silvers challenging Skye and Caerulus. Their riders pushed them to deftly avoid most of the flames from the blue pair and fire their own flames. Yet several hits from the blues slowed the silvers as they squirmed and darted in among the free-flying gold dragons. One of the riders fell off but quickly recovered to fly on its own. The other rider dismounted his silver dragon to fly on his own as well.

Lightening the load, I imagined.

The third silver at the edge of my vision caught my attention as its rider suddenly slapped it with a wing. The silver dragon stopped and hovered in the air while the rider took stock of the battle situation.

I glanced back in time to see the blue couple crank up their flames. One by one, the silvers' bodies close to Skye and Caerulus coiled and their screams bounced off the canyon walls. They writhed as their skin shriveled and peeled off their twisting bodies while they spiraled to the ground. Some of their toasted body parts were headed right toward me. I darted all around the place as the falling debris and dragons dropped near me.

A big shadow flew across the ground coming my way. The other silver! I twirled my slingshot three fast rotations, made a quick judgment about where the silver would be in the next two seconds and released one of the cords of my sling. My two rocks shot to the Heavens.

The rocks hit the silver dragon above me when the silver and his rider were only a few feet from Skye's unguarded back. The silver dragon went limp like a dead squirrel and plunged to the ground toward me. His rider flew clear. I loaded another rock in my sling and whirled it over my head and released it toward the silver's rider who was headed right for me.

I turned to run.

The gold rider came on me too fast. I heard a swishing sound behind like a single dragon wing cutting through the air. A mighty force hit the back of my head and my breath was knocked out of my body as I slammed into the ground.

Darkness.

I could still hear something going on—the sound of a tornado of dragon flames receding into the distance. Then silence for only a moment.

I seemed to move from timelessness to brutal pain all over my body, to the sensation of being covered by dirt and dead grass. Finally, I forced open my eyes. I *was* covered in dirt and grass!

A fire broke out on the ground too close for comfort. I flailed wildly and tried to get up, run, and become fully awake all in one motion. I fell on my face, but bounced up and ran a few steps.

"What? Where am I—"

Then I remembered Skye and Caerulus. Overhead, the two blue dragons turned their attention to gold dragons squealing in fright as they flew off in all directions to avoid another blast of fire. Three of them, nearly tangled in each other's wings, were caught in fresh columns of blue-dragon fire.

The three golds turned black before my eyes and trailed glowing embers like fireworks as they plunged to the ground right at me! Again!

Through the dust and smoke all around, I once again danced like a wild man to keep from getting squashed by one of the dog-sized gold dragons.

This was too much, but to save myself from more disaster, I looked to see if another dragon was falling on my head. Instead, I saw the last gold scurry away, his tail smoking as burned skin fell off.

Now only Skye and Caerulus circled each other, singing something in dragon language that sounded a lot like a joyous victory song. They reached with their front feet, entwined, twisting around and around as they gradually landed.

The fear of something else falling on my head evaporated, and I searched to see what had hit the back of my head earlier. A blackened silver wing still jerked on the ground like a freshly killed chicken. I stomped it in a fit to stop the creepy twitching and to get even with the silver dragon that had tried to kill me as it fell to its death.

Great shot with your sling, Caerulus said as the two blues approached me.

In an instant, I went from mad as all Hades at the golds and silvers to embarrassed. "Yeah? Well, thanks, lots of practice killing squirrels, but—"

Are you OK? Skye asked.

"Sort of... mostly. But what about you two? Where did that fire come from?" At that moment I was excited, yet without warning, I got mad again. This time at them. "How did you do that? Why didn't you use fire before? And why didn't you tell me you could breathe fire again? You could have cooked that hog yourselves. I feel like a dumb kid!"

Calm down, calm down, Caerulus said in a way I wished my father would use when I was angry.

"Well, where in the Blue Dragon Blazes did the sulfur come from? I mean, isn't that what you used to create the flame?" I looked boldly into Skye's golden eyes as if I were her impatient father, and not a whining kid.

No. I didn't tell you about the sulfur because I had forgotten about it over the years. And then... it just came to me that last night in the cave and I remembered about my father's secret cache of sulfur.

I swear, a rather sheepish smile crossed her face. Another impossible expression on a dragon!

When my brothers, sisters, and I were little ones before the humans came to get us, my father feared our capture was destined to happen. The humans were too cunning. He decided to hide a source of sulfur in a small tunnel in our cave. He told us it was there for an emergency.

But a long time passed before the humans finally tricked us and took us away. There was no chance for him to get back to the sulfur. And then that last night you and I spent in the cave, something came to me in a dream that triggered the memory.

Before we left, when you were still asleep, I crept into the cave hoping to remember where he had shown us the hiding place. I couldn't find it and almost gave up. Finally, I thought, 'OK, don't think, just go and follow wherever your nose leads you.' It was hard when the narrow tunnel split in different directions. My tendency to stick to the tighter way must have triggered my memory or maybe I thought Dark Cloud would choose the harder way hoping to fool the nosey humans.

After a while, I lost heart again, but then I came on a pile of rocks from a ceiling collapse covered in a heavy coat of dust. The long-forgotten scent of sulfur came to me in a ribbon of air. I found it!

I thought about that morning in the cave and remembered the feeling she was hiding something from me.

I think she read my thoughts, one of her annoying traits, when she said, *I felt the emergency my father spoke of had come upon us because the silvers and golds were so close to discovering us. I took the sulfur but said nothing because I was afraid I wouldn't know how to use it.*

"OK, good enough, but why didn't you use it when we ambushed the train? Or when the golds came for us in that other cave in the first place? Or even yesterday when we rescued Caerulus and your children in the big barn?

She sighed and said, *In the cave the quarters were too tight and, besides, I hadn't remembered about the sulfur yet. And as far as taking control of the train and getting everyone out of the barn, the situation was not dire enough.*

"Wow, you have a high standard for dire! But yeah, I can kind of see it with taking the train since that wasn't that hard after all."

The other problem, she went on, *was that once used, it would quickly become known and the humans would redouble, no, triple their efforts to recapture Caerulus and me to tamp down the story of what we did. If not, it would threaten their hold on all dragons.*

"Oh, all right, those are all good points. Still... using the sulfur would have made life a lot easier at the time."

Caerulus spoke up. *I was as surprised as you, Jaiden, when Skye told me about the sulfur and then gave me some for my throat pouch right after reuniting with me in my stall. I hardly had a chance to calm down from seeing her again and then, 'Oh by the way, here's some sulfur. Think you can light it up?'*

After a pause, he went on. *Actually, I didn't think could. I had never breathed fire because my family were captives before I was born. But her instructions were very good. Then in this old barn here, she gave me more sulfur in hopes I could spit a strong flame.*

If anything, Skye added, *I knew I could fire mine and still do some damage if he wasn't able to get a good flame going. But, he did just fine, my hero.* She gave him a playful nudge.

Oh sure, he said. *I don't believe that for a minute! But we make a great team. And soon our little ones will learn to fire up and defend themselves and our kind.*

I felt good about that, but... "Now your future depends on stopping these gold and silver dragons. And yet you allowed the one gold to escape?"

We will be long gone before the humans can return to this place, Skye said, *and they won't likely find us in the far north by that time. I know these dragons were sent because of our escape. When that one gold returns wounded and burned, the humans will realize what happened. Then they will think twice before foolishly attacking independent dragons for fear we, once again, possess fire.*

More dragons will get sulfur as more escape, Caerulus said. *The story of our escape cannot be easily silenced. The word will get around and I have a feeling we'll find new sources of sulfur and gladly share the supplies. We won't stay in the north for long.*

And, Skye added, *the story of a human who took a big risk to fight alongside dragons and even kill an attacking silver dragon will encourage other people who feel much the same. You can't be that weird,* she teased.

"I don't know," I muttered. "Just when you think things are going fine, something mucks up the works. I am my father's son when it comes to getting overly enthused and unrealistic about things like this."

Finally, the children must have gained enough courage to peek from the barn to see why all the noise finally stopped. The three squealed as they flew across the open space between the barn and us.

They all babbled at the same time.

Deryn, the female, said *Mommy, Daddy! Are you all right?*

Did you show those nasty little dragons a thing or two? Baldric said.

Jarmil the youngest just flew around in circles, exclaiming, *Yay! Yay!*

Both Skye and Caerulus struggled to nuzzle their children as they danced around and bumped into each other and their parents. Finally, the youngsters accepted neck hugs when both parents wrapped their necks around each child.

I felt a little out of place as the family reunion progressed. But I'm sure everyone was tired and we still had a long way to go before they could breathe freely.

Skye turned to me and walked me toward the barn. *I can take you home as soon as you're ready. I think Caerulus wants to rest, work on his free flying techniques and then start a slow progress of flights to the far north. He doesn't want to tire the young ones, so it'll be slow going.*

"I don't want to take you away from your family just as you have re-united. Drop me off in Portville. I don't think anyone will recognize me if I wear farmer's clothes. Then I can sneak on a train back to a town near Hilltop. I think I've learned how to do that now. And I'm good at hiking the long distance back to home."

I can do better than that, she said.

TWENTY-THREE

Homecoming

Having never seen Hilltop from the air, I thought it would be something like in dreams. But the reality was surprising. All the familiar things that seemed big on the ground were like a collection of kid's toys and pretend fields, barns, and tiny little animals. Even our cow looked like a mouse.

"Over there," I said, "It's the red barn with a garden next to it. Drop me off in the field farther up the slope between those hills where no one will see us."

She landed on the field my father left dormant for the season. I stepped off from the harness and looked her in the eye. She lowered her massive head.

I had one more thing to say to her. "Please come and get me soon. After you and Caerulus begin to spread the word to fellow dragons. I want to see other dragons become free like your family has. *Don't leave me out.*"

Skye looked deeply into my eyes. It felt a little creepy because she was so silent.

I went on, "I've developed a taste for adventure. In a few months, either I'll get my father to come around to accept that I have a higher purpose to help dragons or I'll be ready to leave him in the past and never come back. Besides, at some point the train people might come for me."

You still have some growing up to do. And someday you'll want your own family, she said. *And, I'm not sure what Caerulus and I will do. We're rather tired right now and just want to live somewhere in peace.*

"I know what you mean, but first this great thing needs to happen. Dragons and people should be able to get along. There will be more adventures. And I want to be a part of them."

You already are. She smiled in that weird kind of way that I've discovered only a dragon can do. *The stories about you will grow into legend. But you're right. There is more to do. And there will be new stories.*

"Good. You can tell those stories because you're a good storyteller like your father."

I didn't know what else to say. I began to feel like I was getting in over my head. Farm boys don't usually dream big things for themselves like this. Maybe I was more like my father than I realized.

I couldn't imagine him feeling like he had some big mission to accomplish other than putting food on the table and staying out of trouble. Something to think about. Still, I believe the thrill of adventure now had a hold on me.

"Bye," I said. "Don't forget me."

I won't. Until I see you again.

She rose, her grand wings reaching upward as she launched into the big blue sky—what she was named for—and flew northeast disappearing behind the highest hill beyond our farm.

Footsteps crunched on the rough ground behind me.

I turned.

"Father."

"Jaiden. Are you back to stay?" His voice sounded strange to me, like he spoke through a thick blanket. His eyes watered but he wiped hard at them.

His face darkened. "Where in Hades' name have you been with those—those *dragons?*" He spat the name out and raised his hand ready to whack me.

I backed away one step, then decided I didn't have to act like a little kid. I stood my ground and said, "They're not evil—"

"I couldn't care less. I've been here alone while you were flying all over the place. I heard rumors. Crazy stuff." He regarded me like he would a poisonous snake.

After a moment, he lowered his arm. "I was left here to do all the work, but—"

Then something unexpected happened. His eyes flooded, he wiped left and right, as if angry at such a show of weakness when he was trying to intimidate me.

I mumbled, "I'm sorry for that." I, too, fought to maintain my manhood, such as it was. My father never showed any emotion beyond anger or impatience. Mostly, he seemed as if he didn't feel anything.

After long moments of silence, I said, "I want to stay for a while. I have a lot to tell you. I am not a traitor to humans. There is more to dragons than a bunch of big shot people have told us. The dragons are a lot like us. They want to be free and live in peace with their families."

Dad's eyes bore through me like he was trying to force me to tell the truth and not some big old made-up story.

Out of nowhere, I thought of something to distract him. "Oh yeah, you wouldn't believe the shot I got off with my sling to bring down a silver dragon."

To my surprise, he actually grinned at that news but he glanced away as if he couldn't look me in the eye while he wiped his smile off.

"Gal-darn it, I missed you, son." Maybe I was wrong but I had a strong feeling he meant his voice to sound mad but instead it was a muddle of sadness and anger.

Still, what he said shocked me in spite of the tears in his eyes. I expected a punch in the face or a swift kick.

"I kind of missed you too, Dad. I didn't mean to leave without a word, it just happened and then it was impossible to get back—until now."

He kicked dirt clods with his worn boot. At that moment, I thought he meant those clods to be my face. But maybe it was me that saw anger in most everything he did with me. I started to realize I needed to either stand up for myself or understand why he seemed to be angry most of the time. One way or another, I couldn't walk away from him until we could be honest with each other.

My thoughts scattered when he said, "I believe you. I thought about many things while you were gone. I thought about your mother and how she left us. She didn't want to die. She wanted to raise you and make a home for us. I miss her a lot but I could never talk about it because it hurt so much."

Again, he stomped the ground. I knew this kind of thing made him mad at himself so I stepped toward him and reached for—I don't know. Maybe grip his arm as a comrade, or shake his hand... or what?

It was a crazy thing to do because I couldn't remember either of us touching. I only knew the feel of his hand across the side of my head or his boot on my backside. I half expected a fist in my stomach or his hand pushing me away. But he let me pat his shoulder like we were old buddies or something.

Then he gripped both my arms in a hold so tight I thought I was going to yelp with pain. But I didn't care, it was better than getting punched.

He finally let go and we walked toward the house. I knew better than to say anything more right then. But I wanted to hear about my mother and he seemed ready to talk about her. Yet I couldn't rush him because nothing made him madder than for me to even suggest that he had to do something. It was up to him to talk about my mother again.

Later, there would be time for my Dragon Train story.

I heard voices singing in my head. I glanced sideways at my father. He darted his head around as if looking for something. He heard them, too. Though I couldn't tell if he was fascinated, confused or horrified.

Right then, we turned and saw five blue dragons fly upward from behind the high hill, two adults looking majestic and three youngsters rather awkward as they followed. The five traced a wide circle across the sky.

My mind filled with their joyful voices.

Fly you Blues, Fly.
Reach for the clouds,
Head for the land
Before sunset.
Find your freedom,
Find your comfort,
Find what's needed
To live and love.
Find your own home,
Sing Dragon Songs
To Flight, Fire, Family.
Fly you Blues, Fly!

Caerulus and the three young ones peeled off from Skye and flew beyond our sight behind the big hill.

My father murmured, "I'll be gal-darned, slammed, and pounded."

I shaded my eyes from the sun's glare, watching Skye as she drifted a few more moments flying low near us. She circled once, dipped to wave with her right wing and with a mighty stroke, disappeared over the hills and the Emerald Forest beyond.

The End

ABOUT THE AUTHOR

RJ enjoys writing fantastical stories of all sorts, music, volunteering, and adventure. RJ and his wife spend a lot of time with Trixie—their famous rescue dog—as well as family and friends.

Lightning Source UK Ltd.
Milton Keynes UK
UKHW040824031020
370961UK00001B/43